W9-CAW-324

STRANGE & AMAZING WORLDS
OCEANS

STRANGE & AMAZING WORLDS

OCEANS

Dr Philip Whitfield

Viking

VIKING
Published by the Penguin Group
Viking Penguin Inc., 375 Hudson Street,
New York, NY 10014, U.S.A.
Penguin Books Ltd, 27 Wrights Lane,
London W8 5TZ, England
Penguin Books Australia Ltd, Ringwood,
Victoria, Australia
Penguin Books Canada Ltd, 2801 John Street,
Markham, Ontario, Canada L3R 1B4
Penguin Books (N.Z.) Ltd, 182–190 Wairau Road,
Auckland 10, New Zealand

Penguin Books Ltd, Registered Offices:
Harmondsworth, Middlesex, England

First published in 1991 by Viking Penguin a division of
Penguin Books U.S.A.

STRANGE & AMAZING WORLDS: OCEANS
was conceived, edited and designed by
Marshall Editions
170 Piccadilly
London W1V 9DD

Editor: Fran Jones
Art Editor: Daphne Mattingly
Picture Research: Elizabeth Loving
Editorial Director: Ruth Binney
Production: Barry Baker
Janice Storr
Nikki Ingram

Library of Congress catalog card number: 91-50211
(CIP data available)

ISBN 0-670-84176-5

Typeset by MS Filmsetting Limited, Frome, Somerset
Printed and bound in Spain
by Artes Graficas, Toledo
D.L.TO:598-1991

10 9 8 7 6 5 4 3 2 1

Contents

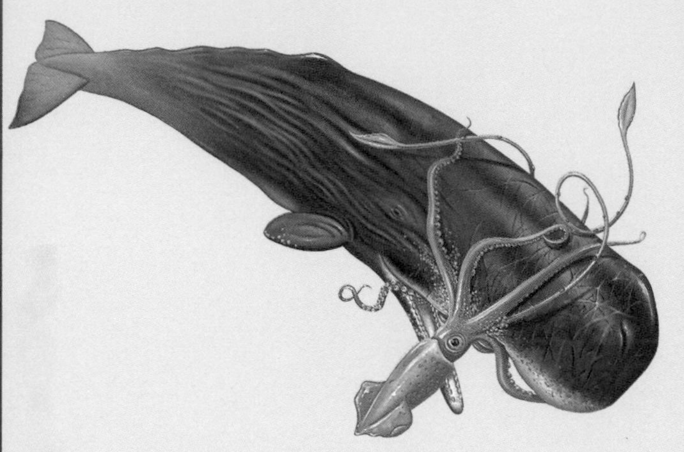

Introduction

The ocean world is strange, amazing, and mysterious. Strange, because people are not designed to live underwater, so it is difficult to imagine the life of, say, a fish or an octopus, lived every minute with water all around. Amazing, because the facts we do know about the sea are mind-boggling; its huge size, its undersea volcanoes taller than Mount Everest, and its ocean valleys which go down deeper below the sea than the tallest mountains stand above it. Mysterious, because the underwater world is full of creatures and happenings that we simply do not understand.

This book takes you into the amazing world of seawater, the salty liquid that covers two-thirds of the surface of our planet. We cannot drink it, and we can swim only on its very surface. But in the oceans, surprising things are common. The oceans are home to the largest animals that have ever lived on Earth, like the blue whales weighing in at almost 150 tons each. Big is normal in the sea.

Scientists believe that four billion years ago, life began in the sea. Down the many ages which have passed since that early time, the life in the sea has become more and more varied – more and more incredible. This book gives a glimpse of the richness and weirdness of these strange and amazing living things. Read about minute plants on which all sea creatures depend for their food and about the "monsters" of the sea like the whales and giant squid. Discover living coral reefs thousands of miles long and tiny animals smaller than a pinhead. Contrast bright red tube worms that only live in the darkest ocean depths with flying fish that skim in the sunlight above the waves.

In the pages that follow you will find out about the incredible ways in which people explore and use the world of the sea with the help of diving suits, submarines, and submersibles. You can learn how fish are caught, how fish farmers are just beginning to "cultivate" fish and other edible sea creatures for food, and how valuable fuels and minerals are brought up from the ocean depths.

The ocean is a world we hardly understand, although more is being discovered by scientists each year. Its strange and amazing stories are never-ending.

THE LANDSCAPE OF THE DEEP

The bottom of the sea is not flat. If all the waters of the oceans were drained away, a wonderful landscape would be seen.

Near the land is the shallow smooth bottom called the continental shelf. From there, the bottom slopes down to the deep ocean floor from which vast volcanoes rise. In other places, steep-sided valleys, called trenches, plunge into the depths.

This landscape is formed because the seabed is not still. Very slow movements of the Earth's crust happen there all the time. Rocks that have melted from the fierce heat deep inside the Earth ooze up through the ocean floor. They spread sideways and harden to form new sea floor. If the hot liquid rock, lava, comes up at one spot, a volcano forms. If the moving seabed slips under a block of land, a valley is made.

▲ *More than 65 percent of the Earth's surface is covered by oceans. All of this seawater provides a home for thousands of different types of plants and animals that are suited to life underwater. Here a school of blue pullers is searching for food.*

▼ *This view shows the undersea world, from the shallow continental shelf to the mid-ocean depths.*

Land – a continent

The shallow waters of the continental shelf

Deep, mid-ocean sea floor

Mid-ocean ridge where new molten rock comes to the surface, solidifies, and moves slowly sideways as new sea-floor rock.

FACT FILE

The island of Hawaii is drifting gently toward Japan because the sea floor is spreading.

If Mount Everest was placed on the sea floor, it would not be as tall as Mauna Loa in Hawaii.

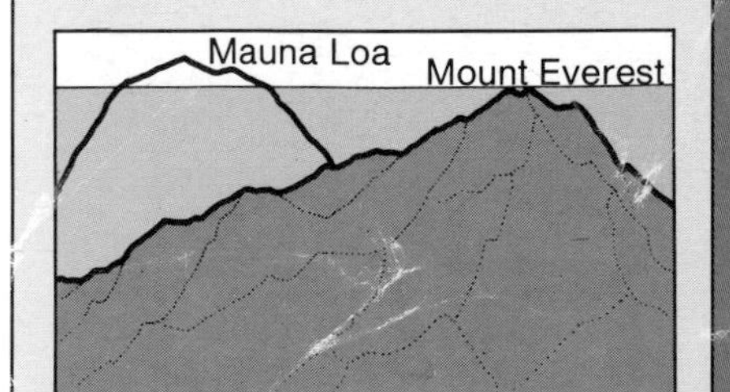

The Marianas Trench in the Pacific Ocean is the deepest undersea valley in the world. It is six times deeper than the Grand Canyon.

▼ *The Hawaiian Islands are volcanic islands formed in mid-ocean. All their rocks are made of lava. Some of their beach sand, made from ground-up lava, is black.*

▲ *New volcanic islands are forming all the time under the sea. This one is Surtsey, and it is growing up just off the coast of Iceland. When the volcanic activity reaches above sea level, the lava cools, becomes solid, and forms an island.*

LIFE AT THE SEA'S EDGE

The seashore is the fascinating place where land and ocean meet. Because the tides come in and out twice a day, living things on a shore have a difficult life – some of the time they are plunged underwater; other times, they are left in the Sun or the cold night air.

This means that all life on a rocky shore has to find a way of clinging on when waves push and pull them. Seaweeds have tough rootlike bases called holdfasts. Mussels tie themselves down with a "beard" of strong threads. Barnacles stick themselves to rocks with a special cement, while starfish and sea urchins hang on with hundreds of tiny tubular feet, each tipped with a suction disk.

The seashore is a zone bursting with life, although sometimes the life is not easy to see at first. On a sandy or muddy shore, for instance, most worms, shellfish, and other animals are hidden underground. Seaweeds and sea creatures are easier to pick out on rocky shores, where they attach themselves to rocks out in the open, or in pools left behind when the tide goes out.

▲ *This beautifully colored seashore creature is a squat lobster and is related to shrimp and crabs. It is well suited to life in rock crevices and pools on the shore where it scavenges for food with its feelers and big claws. The purple color on the rocks is a strange plant – a seaweed that plasters itself over the rock like a layer of purple paint.*

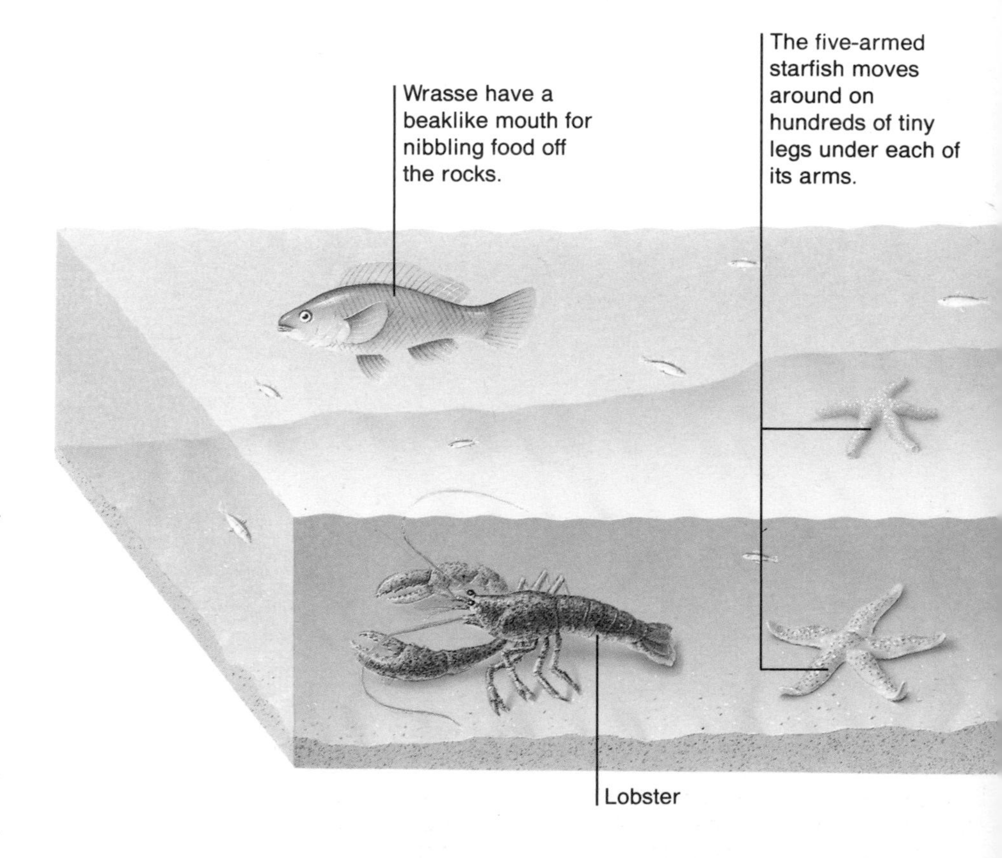

► *This cutaway picture shows the animals and plants living on a rocky shoreline. All shorelines have different zones up and down the beach, which are caused by the movement of the tides.*

At the bottom of the shore, animals and plants are best suited to life under the sea. Life at the top of the shore is specially designed to survive long periods in the air. The zones in between have animals and plants that can do well above and below water.

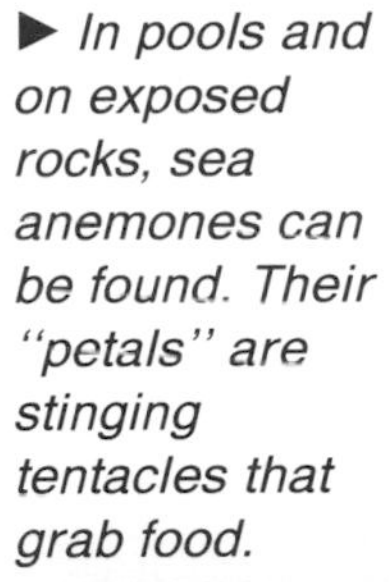

► *In pools and on exposed rocks, sea anemones can be found. Their "petals" are stinging tentacles that grab food.*

◄ *Winkles cruise over the rock surfaces scraping off food with a rough tongue which is hidden under their shell.*

FACT FILE

Limpets are seashore animals that can navigate. Each one always returns to exactly the same small hollow in the rock just before the tide goes out.

A starfish feeds by pulling apart the shells of a mussel. You would not be strong enough to do it yourself.

Lobsters have tough shells that do not grow with the rest of their body. During its first year, a lobster may shed its shell and grow a new one 15 times.

Barnacles stick themselves down on the rocks and wait for the incoming tide to bring them their food.

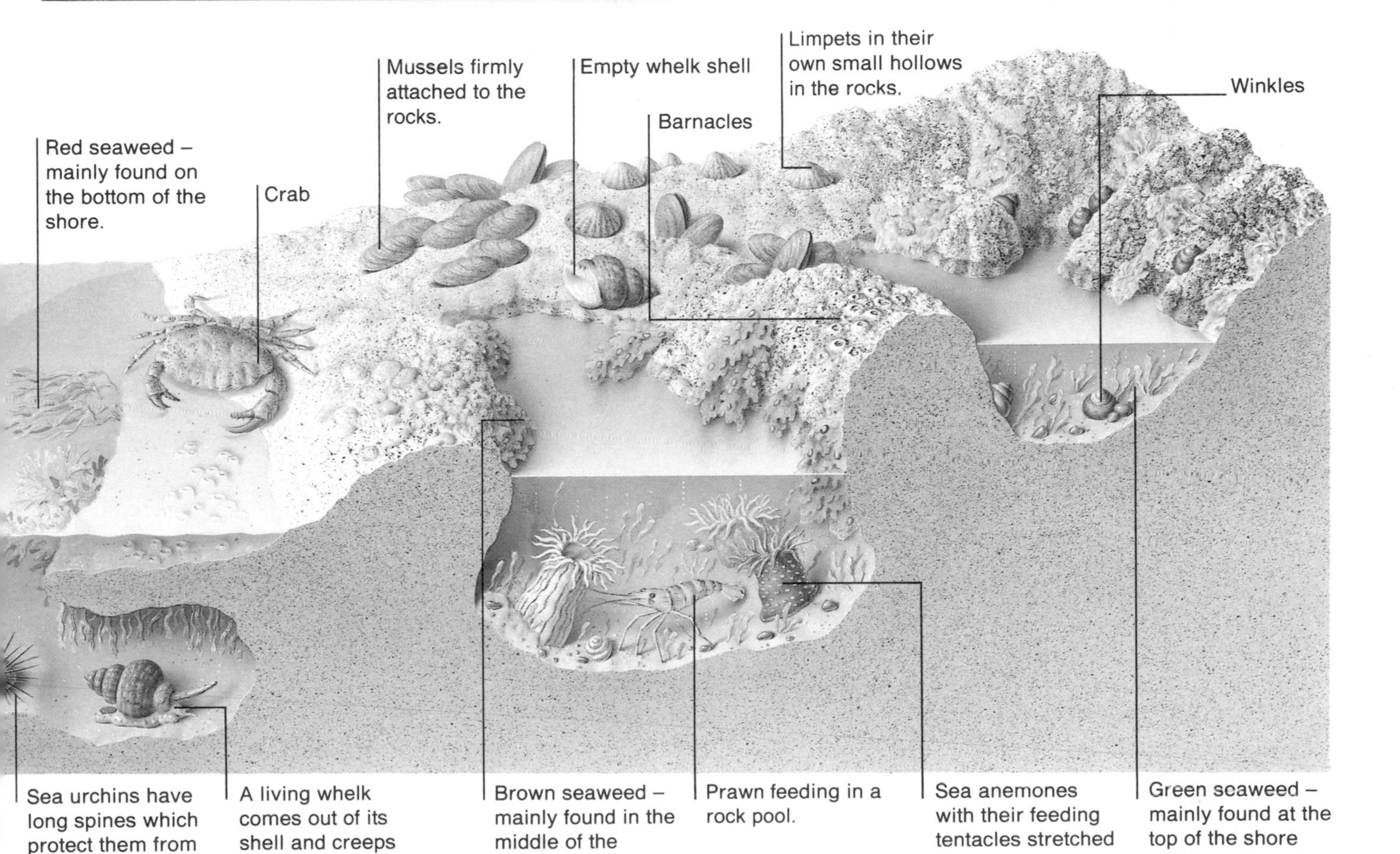

THE OCEAN'S SUNLIT ZONE

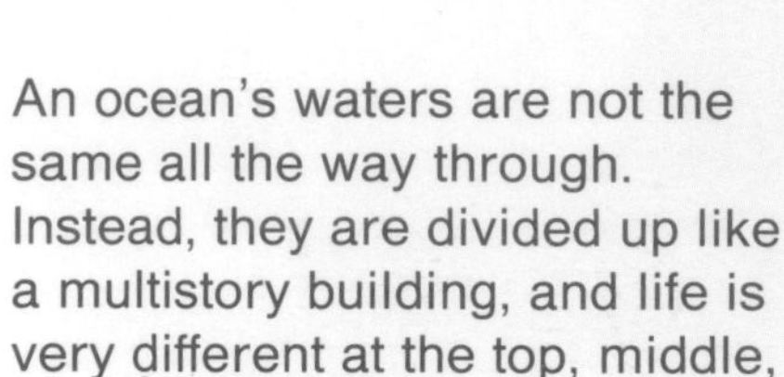

An ocean's waters are not the same all the way through. Instead, they are divided up like a multistory building, and life is very different at the top, middle, and bottom of the seas.

The upper layer of the ocean is warmer than the waters underneath. About 600 feet (200 meters) below the surface, there is a sudden drop in temperature; and from there to the ocean's bottom, it is very cold. The sunlit waters near the top are a perfect place for microscopic plants called plankton to grow. These minute living things are eaten by the tiny animal plankton, and so they start off the food chain for everything else in the sea.

Huge schools of fish, like herring, sardines, pilchards, and anchovies, cruise these waters to eat the animal plankton. Big, fast-swimming fish, like tuna, swordfish, and marlin, streak through the same levels to capture the smaller fish. The plankton is an invitation for all these other creatures to visit the sunlit upper waters.

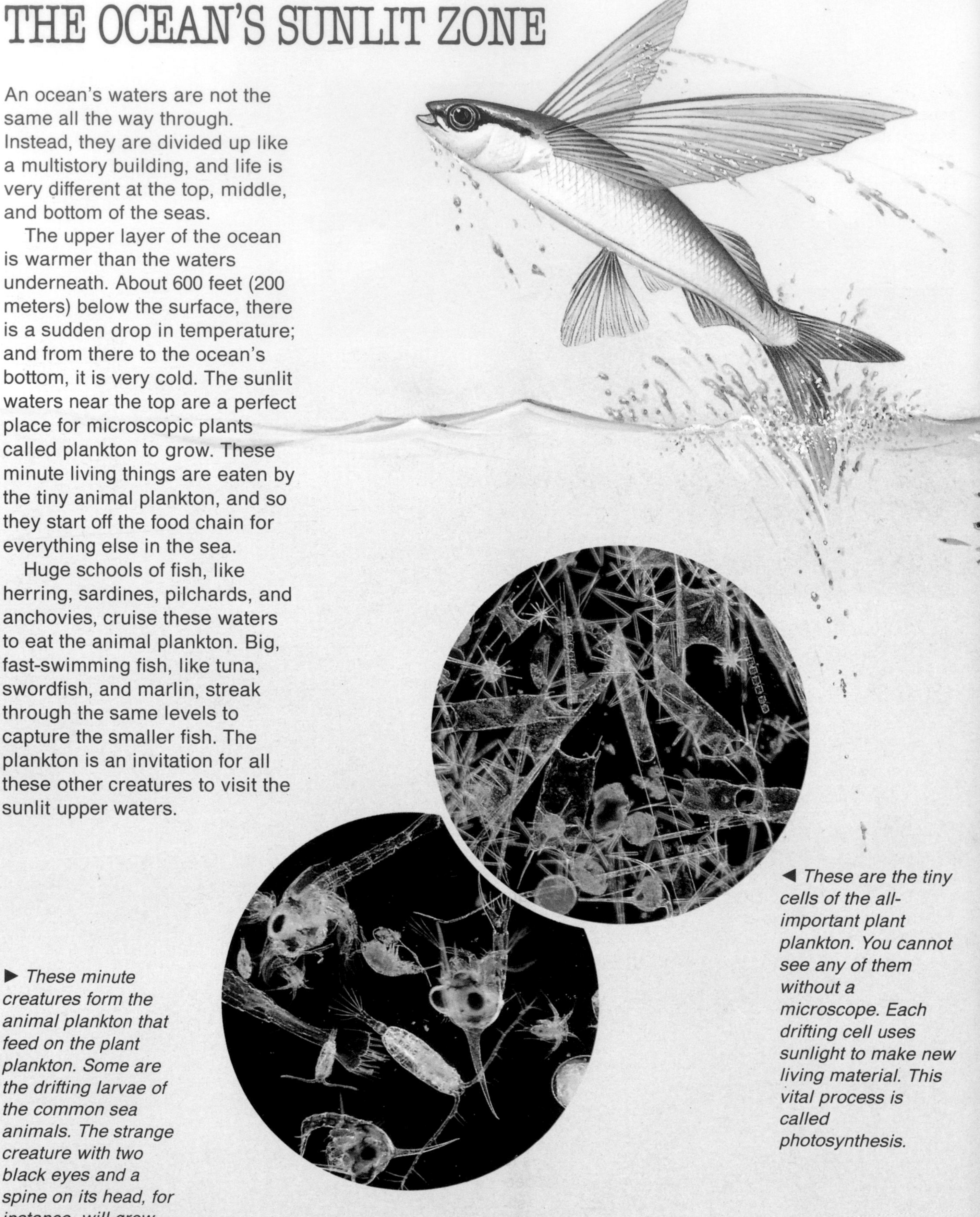

◀ *These are the tiny cells of the all-important plant plankton. You cannot see any of them without a microscope. Each drifting cell uses sunlight to make new living material. This vital process is called photosynthesis.*

▶ *These minute creatures form the animal plankton that feed on the plant plankton. Some are the drifting larvae of the common sea animals. The strange creature with two black eyes and a spine on its head, for instance, will grow into an ordinary shore crab.*

▼ *Life in the upper layers of the ocean can be dangerous. A flying fish glides out of the water on its winglike fins to escape from fish hunting it. A school of young herring speeds through the sunlit water, while a Portuguese man-of-war jellyfish floats on the surface with its tentacles dangling down to kill and catch fish.*

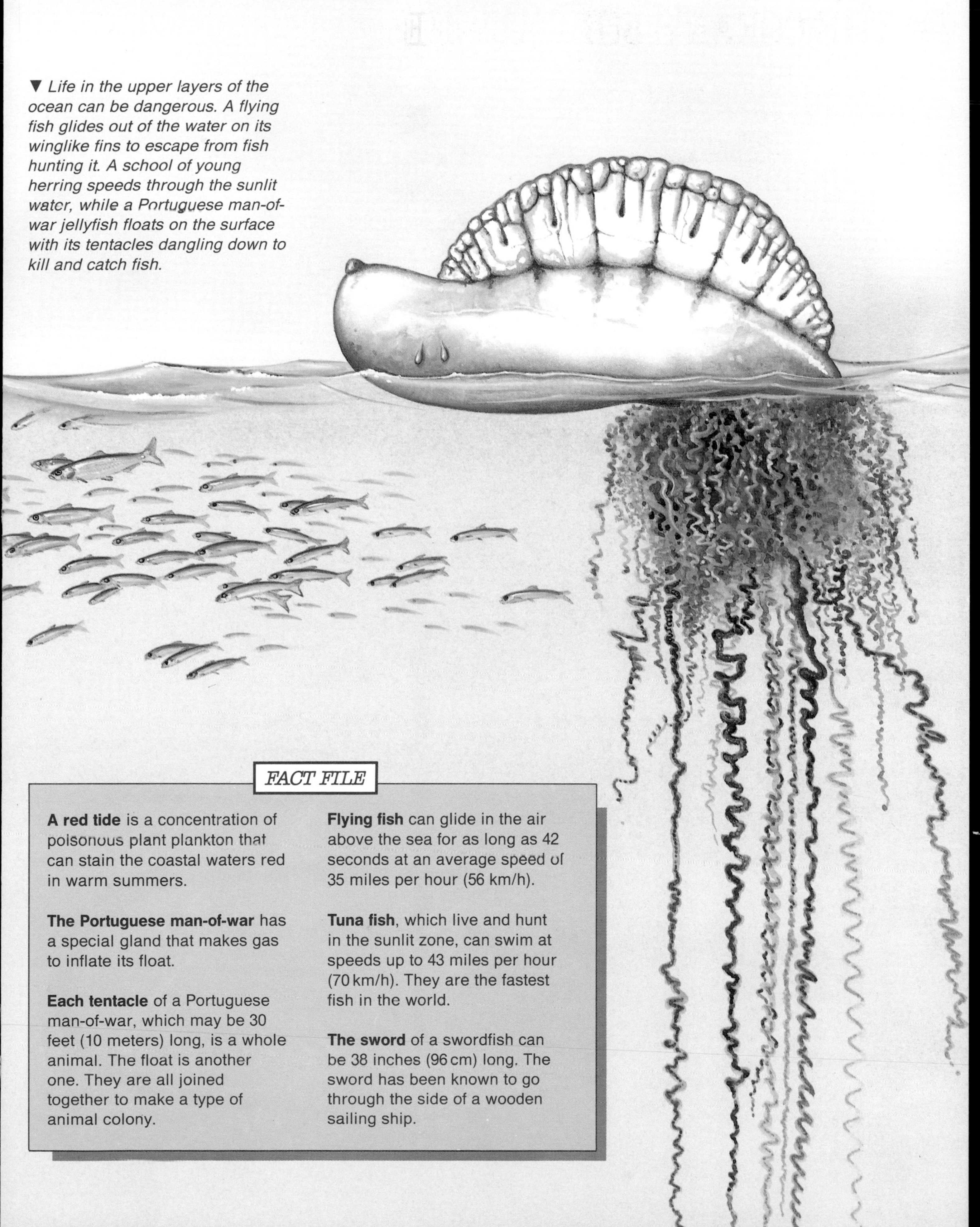

FACT FILE

A red tide is a concentration of poisonous plant plankton that can stain the coastal waters red in warm summers.

The Portuguese man-of-war has a special gland that makes gas to inflate its float.

Each tentacle of a Portuguese man-of-war, which may be 30 feet (10 meters) long, is a whole animal. The float is another one. They are all joined together to make a type of animal colony.

Flying fish can glide in the air above the sea for as long as 42 seconds at an average speed of 35 miles per hour (56 km/h).

Tuna fish, which live and hunt in the sunlit zone, can swim at speeds up to 43 miles per hour (70 km/h). They are the fastest fish in the world.

The sword of a swordfish can be 38 inches (96 cm) long. The sword has been known to go through the side of a wooden sailing ship.

THE OCEAN'S MIDWATERS

The water of the sunlit zone of the oceans is clear and bright. Below it is a very dimly lit twilight world, and then complete, cold blackness.

Utter ocean darkness usually begins at a depth of about 3,280 feet (1,000 meters). Down there, no plants can live because they must have light. All that can be found are animals hunting and feeding on other animals.

To survive in very dim light or complete darkness, fish have developed super-efficient senses. These may be sharp eyes, great sensitivity to tiny vibrations in the water, or a special ability to sense food at great distances by an underwater sense of smell.

This is also the zone of deep-diving whales hunting for food, and of schools of squid zooming around using water-driven jet propulsion. Because it is dark, fish often carry lights on their bodies. These lights are living parts of the fishes' bodies. The light they give out is made by chemical reactions that produce a cold, greenish glow. The fish use the lights either for finding their mates or to confuse animals that try to hunt them in the murky half light.

► *Growing up to 60 feet (20 meters) in length, sperm whales are the biggest of the toothed whales which hunt large prey. They dive to 3,600 feet (1,100 meters) to capture giant squid.*

► *The **coelacanth** is called a living fossil. It is the only living member of a group of fish that died out 90 million years ago.*

▼ ***Lanternfish** make a living in the twilight midwaters of the ocean. Their bodies are studded with living lights. These are designed to confuse the fish that are trying to hunt them.*

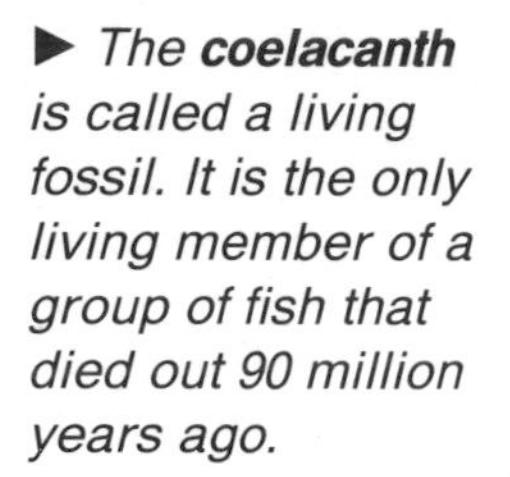

◄ ***Hatchetfish** have differing patterns of lights on their undersides. They identify their mates by using these "neon" signs. Extra-large eyes gaze upward in search of food.*

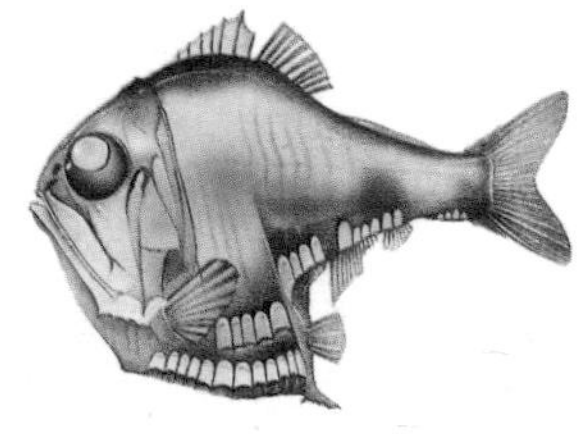

▲ ***Snipe eels** are deep-water fish with very thin bodies up to 4 feet (just over 1 meter) long. Their jaws are filled with small backward-pointing teeth for catching small animal prey.*

▲ ***Walleye pollock** are members of the cod family. They have extra-large eyes to find food in the murky light.*

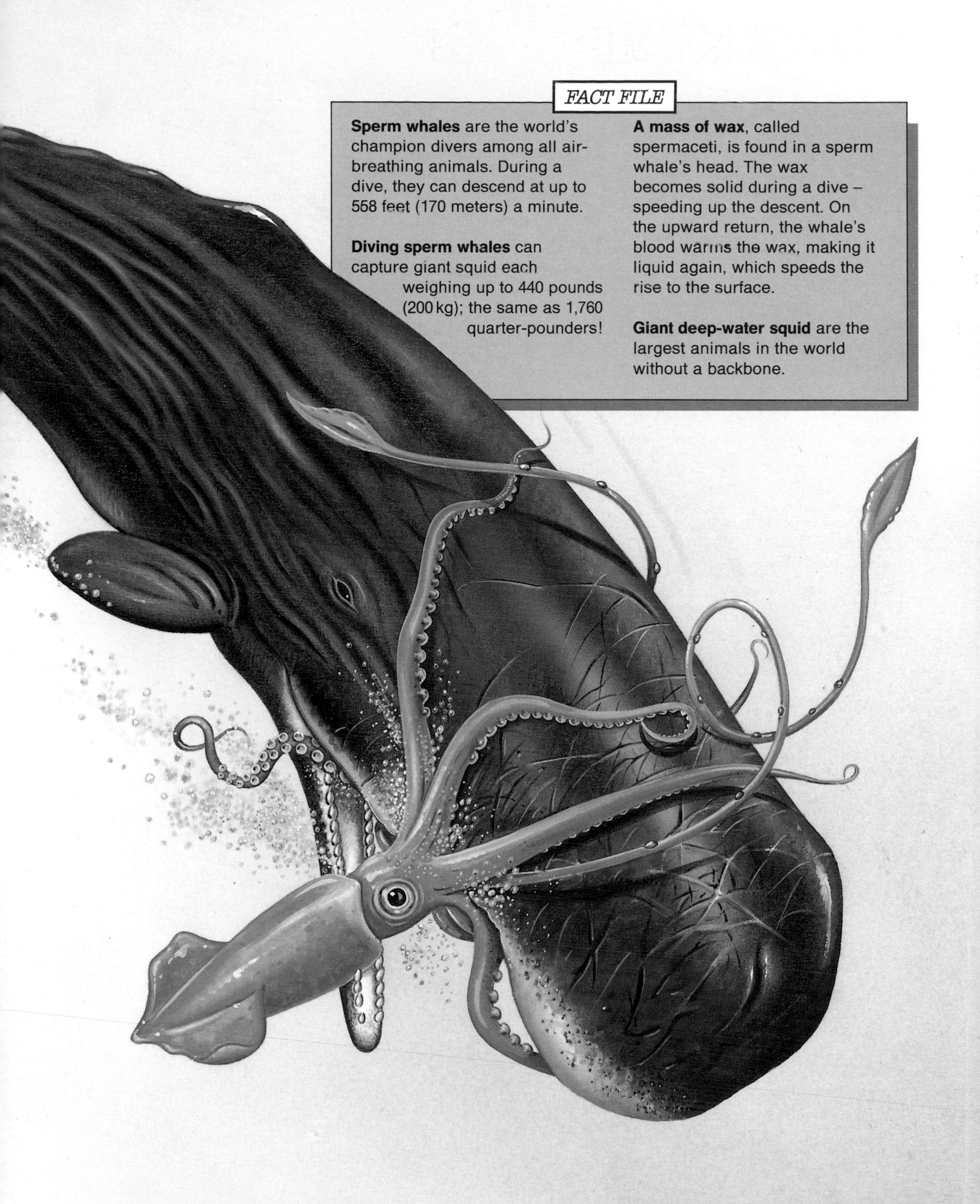

FACT FILE

Sperm whales are the world's champion divers among all air-breathing animals. During a dive, they can descend at up to 558 feet (170 meters) a minute.

Diving sperm whales can capture giant squid each weighing up to 440 pounds (200 kg); the same as 1,760 quarter-pounders!

A mass of wax, called spermaceti, is found in a sperm whale's head. The wax becomes solid during a dive – speeding up the descent. On the upward return, the whale's blood warms the wax, making it liquid again, which speeds the rise to the surface.

Giant deep-water squid are the largest animals in the world without a backbone.

THE SEA BOTTOM

Down on the ocean floor, it is black and cold. The bottom is covered in fine, soft mud called silt or sediment. On or just above the sediment, many types of animals live out their lives feeding on tiny food particles in the water or by eating each other.

Sponges, sea pens, and sea lilies are examples of the sea life that filter small creatures from the water that flows past them. Sponges pull the water through their space-filled bodies, while the sea pens and sea lilies hold out their tentacles or arms to catch food in the current.

Several bottom-living fish have huge mouths, stuffed with long, sharp teeth. To lure prey toward them, angler fish dangle a shining bait in front of their mouths, like an angler with a fishing rod waiting for a catch.

FACT FILE

The gulper eel is not a strong swimmer. It lures prey with a red light at the end of its long tail, then opens its enormous mouth and gulps its meal.

Vampire squid have a web that stretches between their eight main tentacles. It looks like a bat's wing and has given these squid their name.

Hagfish are primitive fishlike animals that have no jaws. Instead they suck out the insides of dead fish which drop down onto the seabed.

A brittle star's arms can be 50 times longer than its body. If an arm snaps off – they are brittle – it will grow again.

◀ *Sea cucumbers are soft-bodied relatives of the spiny sea urchins and starfish. They crawl on the bottom mud and use feeding tentacles to gather tiny food particles.*

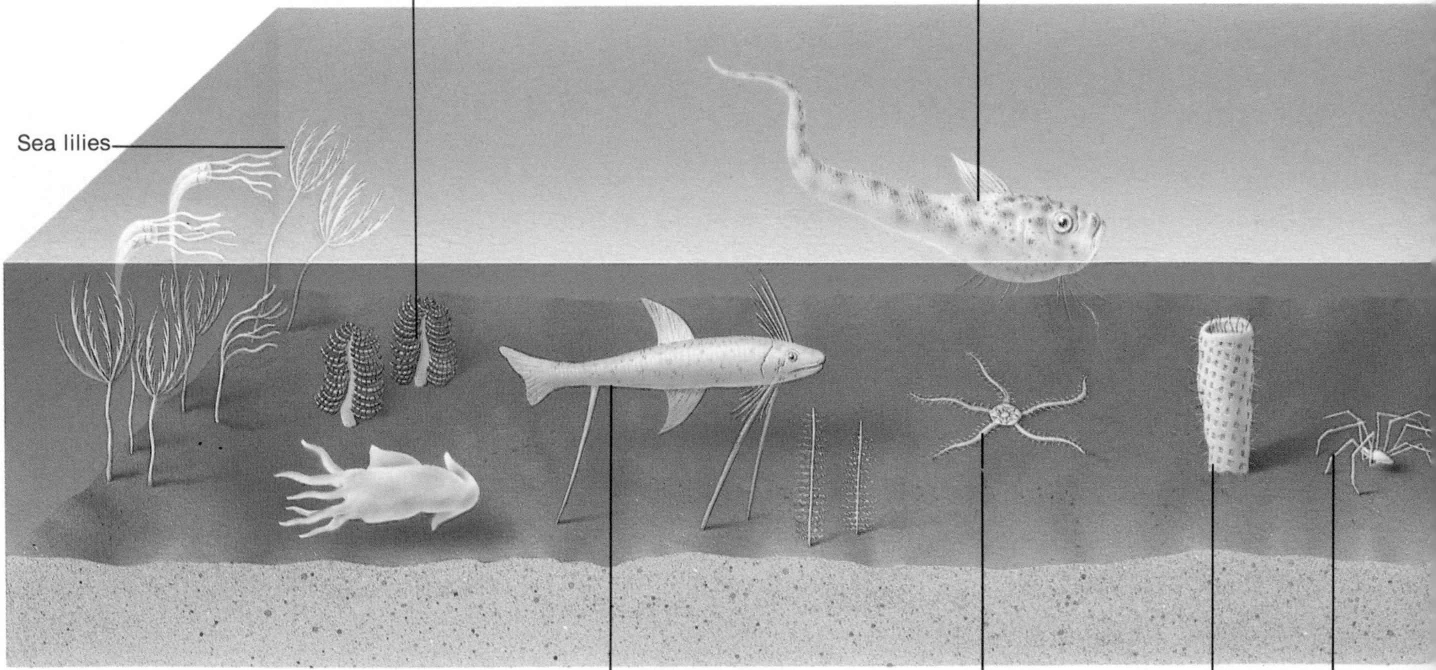

◀ *This fish, called* Pseudoscopelus, *searches for fish prey in the darkness with its huge eyes. It catches them with a mouth full of curved, needle-sharp teeth.*

▼ *The sea bottom in deep parts of oceans looks flat and empty of life. But when any animal dies, or food drops down from above, many types of fish and other creatures gather to eat it. This artwork has more animals in it than would really be seen in one place, but it shows how many different sea-bottom animals there are.*

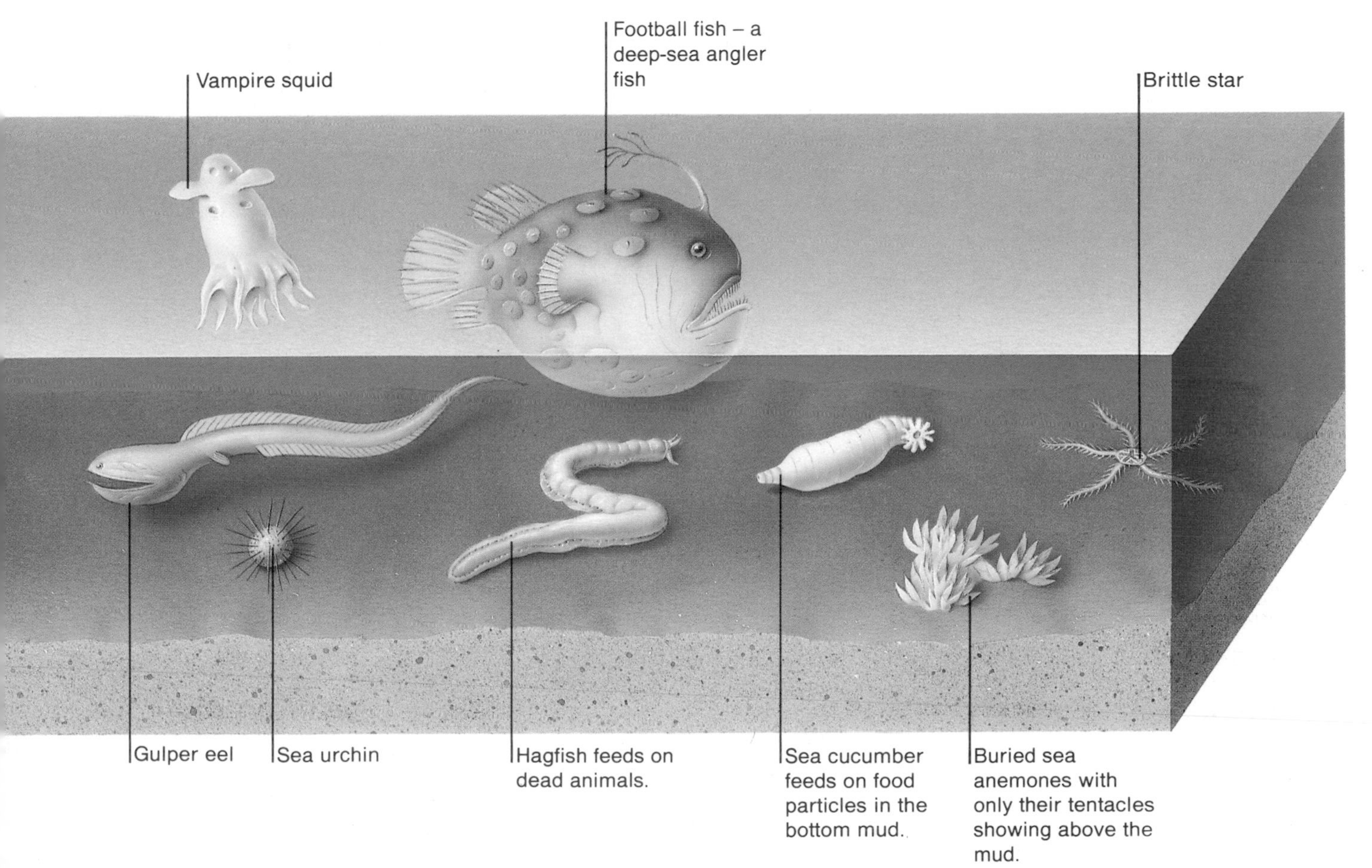

METHODS OF MOVEMENT

Land animals move easily through air which does not slow them down. For sea creatures active life is quite different. They have to move through seawater which is hundreds of times thicker than air. A sea animal has to push itself through water in order to move.

Different creatures in the oceans use many different ways to swim, creep, or glide through water. Fish are able to swim by bending their bodies into waves. They have flattened fins and tails that push against the water like oar blades, which converts these body waves into forward movement.

Whales and dolphins are mammals which swim in a very fish-like way except for one important difference. Because their ancestors lived on the land they developed tails which moved up and down. Watch a dolphin in a dolphinarium and see how it waves its tail up and down rather than side to side like a fish does.

Squids and octopuses move in a completely different way. They use a type of jet propulsion – shooting water out through a nozzle to force themselves along. Jellyfish make a jet in another way, by opening and closing their umbrella-shaped bodies to "lift" themselves through the water.

Bottom-living sea animals creep or walk about. Sea slugs, winkles, limpets, and whelks creep on a single flat piece of muscle called a foot. Ripples pass along the foot which lets these animals glide smoothly forward just like a land snail.

▲ These goldfish (different from the freshwater goldfish in tanks) live in the Red Sea. The size of their tail fins is the clue to their swimming speed – in this case medium-to-fast.

FACT FILE

The seahorse is a fish whose tail is not used for swimming at all. It is a thin, coiled tail used to attach the fish to seaweed, like a monkey's tail holds onto a branch.

Some shellfish like scallops escape from starfish which try to eat them by flapping their shells together. This lets them "fly" through the water.

Penguins swim underwater using their flipper-like wings. The feathers on these wings have become tiny and closely overlapping – just like fish scales. The birds steer underwater by moving their trailing feet.

◀ Three squids power through the sea. They swim backward trailing their tentacles behind them by shooting water out through a pump called a mantle.

◀ *Starfish walk about on hundreds of legs called tube feet. The end of each one has a sticky sucker which pulls the animal forward.*

▼ *Butterfly fish are medium speed swimmers but have small tail fins.*

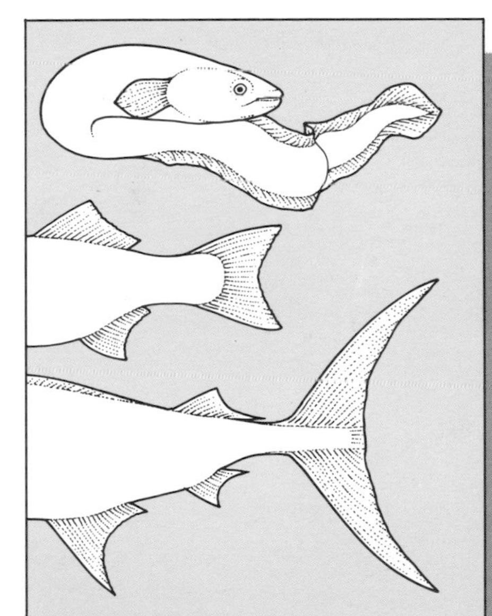

A FISHY TAIL

Small tail fins are found in slow swimmers like the eel. The tail of the bass is linked with a medium-to-fast swimming speed. Long pointed tail lobes, like those on the marlin, are only found on fast swimmers.

DANGER IN THE DEPTHS

Many sea creatures are armed with poisonous or dangerous weapons to protect themselves when threatened.

The weapons of these harmful animals can be sharp spines, with or without poison on them. They may be fearsome stinging cells that cling and inject poison, or massive electric shocks delivered to stun or kill an attacker. Dangerous sea urchins and fish like stonefish, lionfish, scorpionfish, and pufferfish all have spines. Often, these spines have poison glands alongside them, so that when the spine sinks in, it takes poison with it.

Some of these dangerous sea creatures can harm or even kill humans with poisons that can damage the blood or stop the muscles working so that it is impossible to breathe.

The stingray, a cousin of the sharks because it has a skeleton made of gristle (cartilage), can be very dangerous. When disturbed, the ray swings its thin tail right over its head and pushes a bony spine on the tail into its target along with poison. Sharp edges along the ray's spine can also cause nasty cuts.

▲ *Angry or threatened pufferfish can swell up to two or three times their normal size to frighten other fish. They also contain a poison more deadly than cyanide.*

▼ *The electric ray has developed special electrical organs which let it deliver powerful electric shocks. It stops food fishes from moving by wrapping them in its side fins and stunning them with a shock of 200 volts before eating them.*

► *Sea wasps are small jellyfish that kill as many people as sharks do. They do this with the powerful stinging cells in their four clusters of tentacles. Tucked tightly inside each cell is a long, barbed, hollow thread.*

When a prey animal or a person touches a tentacle, the threads rapidly shoot out and impale the target. At the same time, powerful poisons are injected down the hollow thread. The poison can kill.

FACT FILE

Sea snakes can stay underwater for up to two hours. They can bite and inject the most toxic snake venom in the world.

Stonefish rest on the sea bottom and look quite harmless. If you step on one, it will inject a deadly poison.

Stingrays can grow to an enormous size. From tip to tip, their "wings" can measure 10 feet (3 meters).

Witch doctors in the Caribbean have used potions containing pufferfish venom to poison people. Victims turn into a state of robot-like obedience – they become zombies.

Dazzling but deadly, the blue-ringed octopus lives off the coasts of Australia. It flashes bright blue markings when frightened. Do not be tempted to pick one up. Its poisonous bite could kill you .

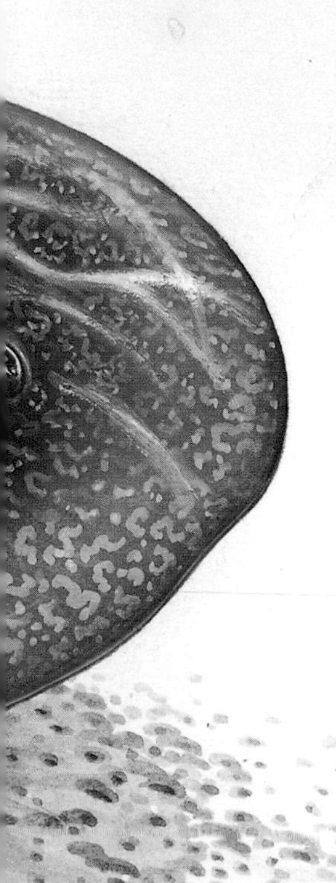

◄ *One of the fears of swimmers in the Mediterranean is treading on a poisonous, spiny sea urchin. They live on sand or rock surfaces and are covered in long, sharp, brittle spines which break off in human flesh if they are stepped on. Poisons on the spines mean the wound is very painful.*

MARINE MIMICS

In the battle to catch food or to keep themselves from being eaten as food under the sea, many animals have become experts at camouflage. By an incredible variety of tricks, these animals are able to blend into the underwater landscape and "disappear." By being camouflage experts, the hunting animals avoid being seen by the prey they are trying to catch, and the hunted animals make themselves much more difficult to find.

▲ *This sargassum fish can hardly be seen at all among the sargassum weeds that give it its name. It is the same color and has seaweed-lookalike frills on its skin.*

► *The longlure frogfish is found in shallow waters in the Caribbean. Its skin texture and color make it blend in perfectly with the seaweed-covered rocks on which it sits.*

The tricks used by sea creatures include strange shapes which somehow match the shape of their surroundings. Some thin and spiky clingfish, for instance, hide head-down among the black spines of sea urchins. They look so similar, they cannot be seen.

Color can be a great help in camouflage. Some fish permanently match the color of their surroundings, or have body shading that makes them difficult to see. Other fish, like flounders and frogfish – and also those masters of disguise, the squid, cuttlefish, and octopus – can actually change their color to fit in with the surroundings. This means that their color and patterning change from minute to minute as they move from place to place. A flounder will even attempt to match a checkerboard background.

TWO-TONE FISH

The patterning on most ordinary-shaped fish that swim in midwater is nearly always the same – they are dark on top and lighter underneath. This "two-tone" pattern helps them to blend in with their background.

In the picture on the right, a mackerel is swimming in midwater. Think of the view that a hunting fish would get if it approached from above or below. From above, it would see a dark back against the dark sea depths. From below, it would see the silvery underside against the bright, shining surface of the sea. From every angle, the fish would be difficult to see.

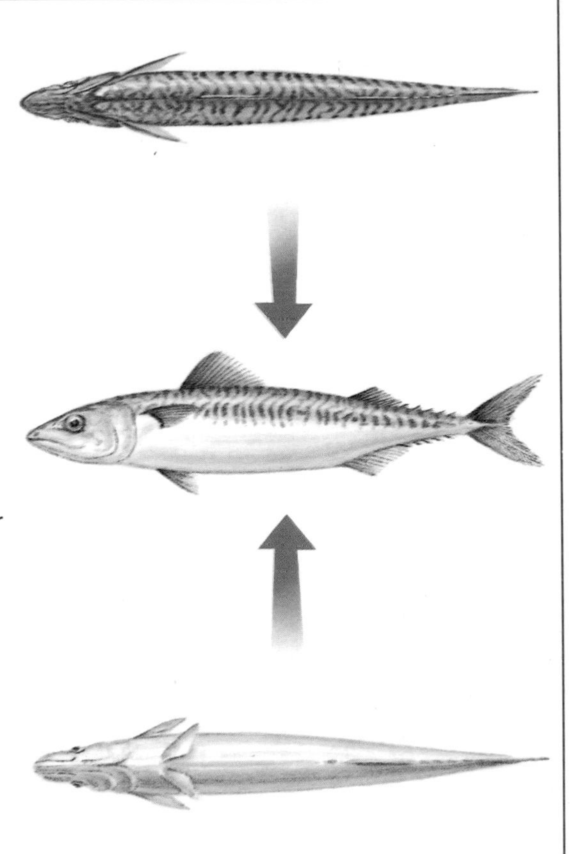

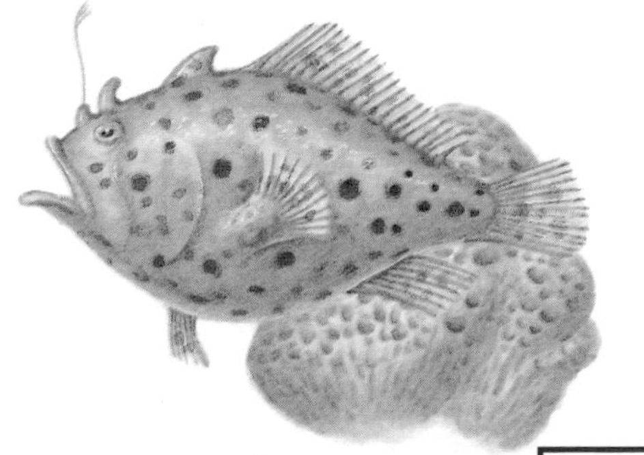

▲ *Frogfish use camouflage both to hide from, and attack, other fish. To hide, they make their odd-shaped bodies the color of the rocks, weed, or coral on which they are sitting.*

To attack, when a food fish comes near, the frogfish wiggles a "copy" of a small fish at the front end of the top fin. This copy, or lure, attracts the prey close enough to be eaten.

FACT FILE

Penguins, which swim underwater, are counter-shaded like fish – dark on their backs, white underneath.

Many sea creatures leave parts of their bodies behind while they escape. **Brittle stars** drop an arm, **octopuses** shoot out a blob of ink, and **sea cucumbers** release a squirming ball of tubes from their gut.

Octopuses can change color in a flash. Special color sacs in the skin get bigger or smaller so that one color shows more and alters the animal's color.

Carpet sharks look like large, flat rocks overgrown with seaweed. All they have to do is lie on the sea floor and eat other fish which swim by without seeing them.

STRANGE PARTNERS

When two different sorts of living things are found together in the sea, it is often because one is trying to eat the other. Dolphins are found near schools of mackerel because they are trying to catch them.

Sometimes, though, the creatures found together seem to be helping one another in some way. This type of "You scratch my back; I'll scratch yours" partnership is called symbiosis. Many extraordinary examples exist in the sea between big animals, small ones, and even plants and microbes. But the creatures always get along better together than they do apart.

There are many advantages to life with a partner. Some animals get protection – like the fish that live among sea anemone tentacles. Others get food, like the giant clams that have sugar-making plant cells in their tissues.

In fact, these types of close animal-plant partnerships are common in the sea. Coral polyps contain plant cells that provide them with food and also help them make their rocky skeletons.

A green worm called *Convoluta* is another plant-animal. It lives on sandy beaches. At low tide it crawls on the beach to bask in the Sun. It gets all its food from the photosynthesis of the green plant cells in its body. It feeds while it sunbathes. When the tide comes in, the worm burrows in the sand to avoid being washed away.

Other partnerships give one of the animals a place to live. Some small goby fish team up with blind shrimp that are good at digging sand tunnels. The two animals share the tunnel and the sharp-eyed fish acts as a sentry for the blind shrimp.

FACT FILE

The living lights on the surface of some deep-sea fish are made by microbe partners. The light organs contain clusters of microscopic, light-producing bacteria.

Hermit crabs which live in empty shells can carry a sea anemone partner on top of their homes. The anemone's stinging tentacles protect the crab from attack.

Cleaner shrimp nearly always have bright-banded bodies of white and orange so that the fish they clean can recognize them.

Clownfish living with sea anemones may hide safely in the gut of the anemone when threatened by large fish.

Decorator crabs camouflage themselves by carefully placing living pieces of sponge and seaweed on their shells.

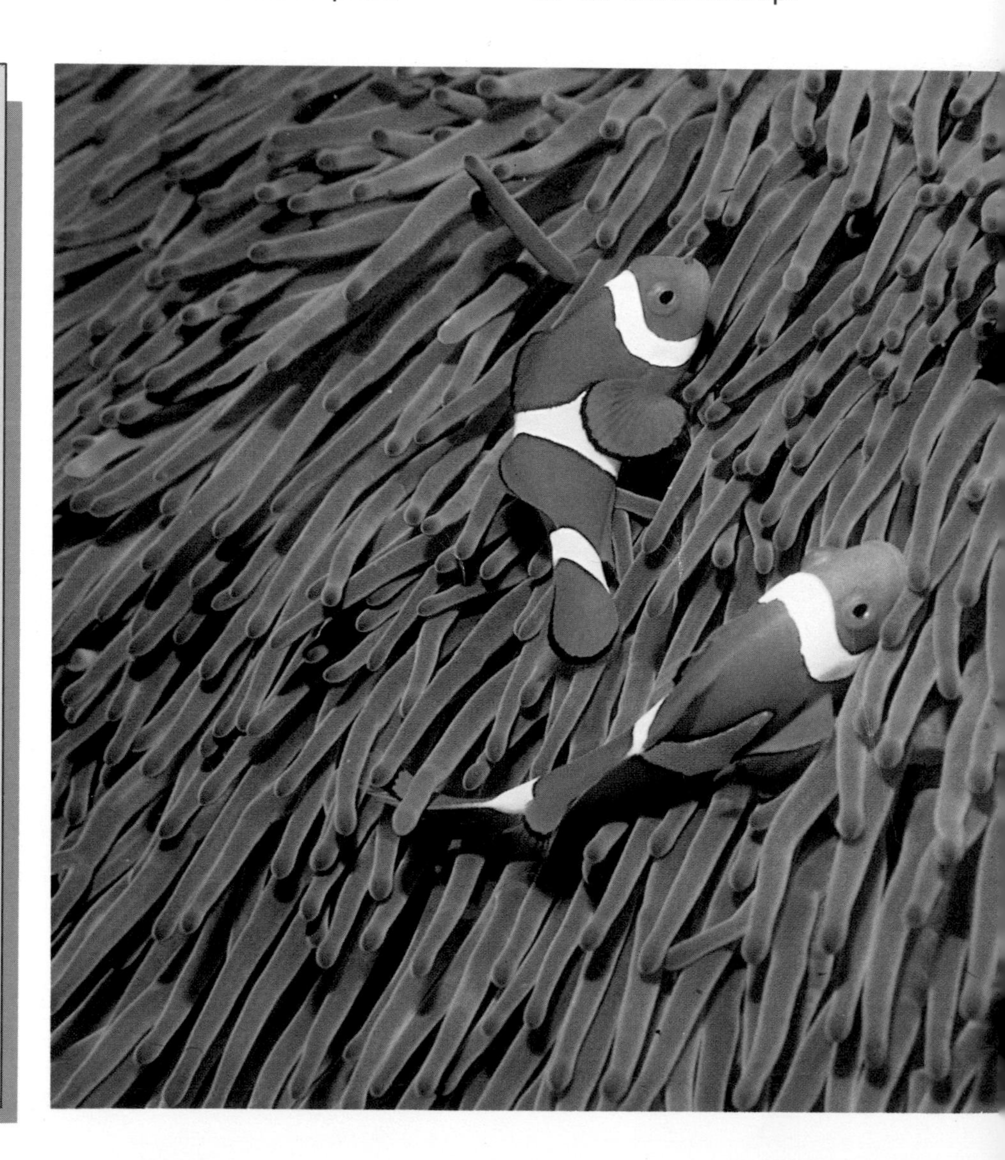

THE GREAT PRETENDER
The real cleaner wrasse shown in the photograph is getting debris out of the mouth of a much larger coral trout. The cleaners eat the parasites and dead scales that they remove. Cleaner fish are usually strikingly marked and put on special displays so that the larger fish recognize them.

Big fish do not usually attack cleaner wrasse that clean up their skin. But the saber-toothed blenny (left, below) is patterned to look like a cleaner wrasse (right, below). Disguised in this way, it can go up to a large fish without being attacked. Instead of cleaning the large fish, the blenny zooms in, uses its saber teeth to bite a piece out of the fish's fins, then swims quickly away!

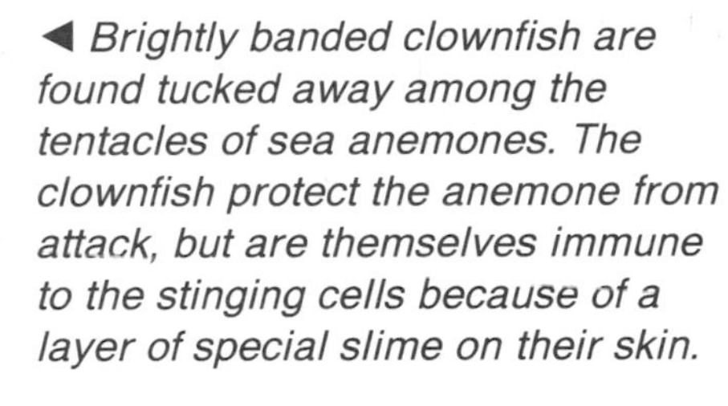

◀ *Brightly banded clownfish are found tucked away among the tentacles of sea anemones. The clownfish protect the anemone from attack, but are themselves immune to the stinging cells because of a layer of special slime on their skin.*

▼ *Giant clams are huge shellfish that catch hardly any food for themselves. In large folds of tissue, they cultivate millions of plant-cell partners. The folds are held in the sunlight so that the plants can make food for the clam.*

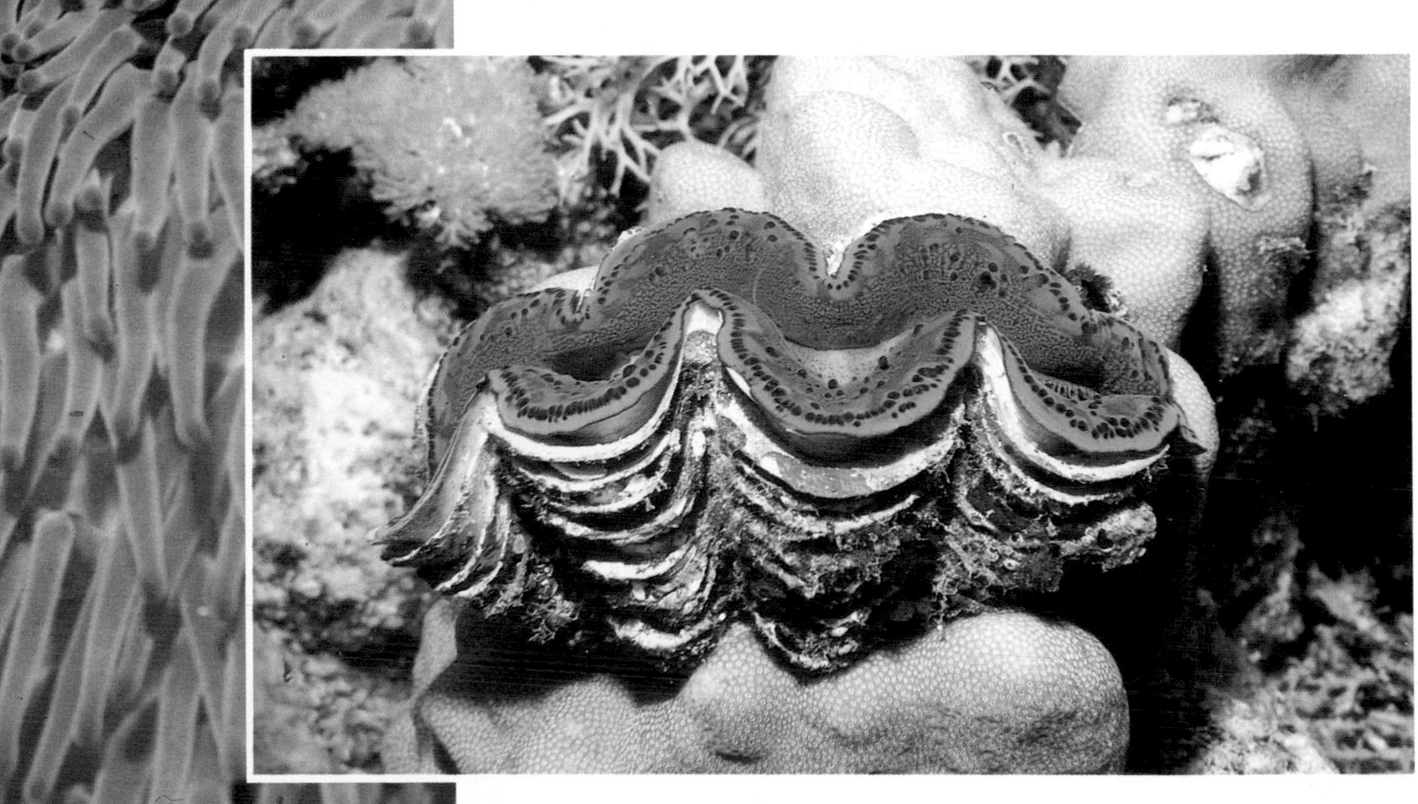

AN OCEAN FULL OF FOOD

The oceans are teeming with food. From the tiniest plants and animals of the plankton – so small that more than a thousand would fit on the head of a pin – to the largest fish, almost everything that lives in the sea can be food for something else.

Nearly every scrap of this living food comes, in the end, from the energy that is given out by the Sun. All the plants of the sea, and especially the minute plant plankton cells, trap

FACT FILE

Sea squirts squirt fluid when touched. It comes out of the holes through which they pass seawater to filter out their food.

Sea urchins scrape their plant food off rocks with a five-jawed mouth that looks like a drill chuck on an electric drill.

Skimmers are seagull-like birds that fly just above the ocean with the lower half of their beaks plowing through the water to catch fish.

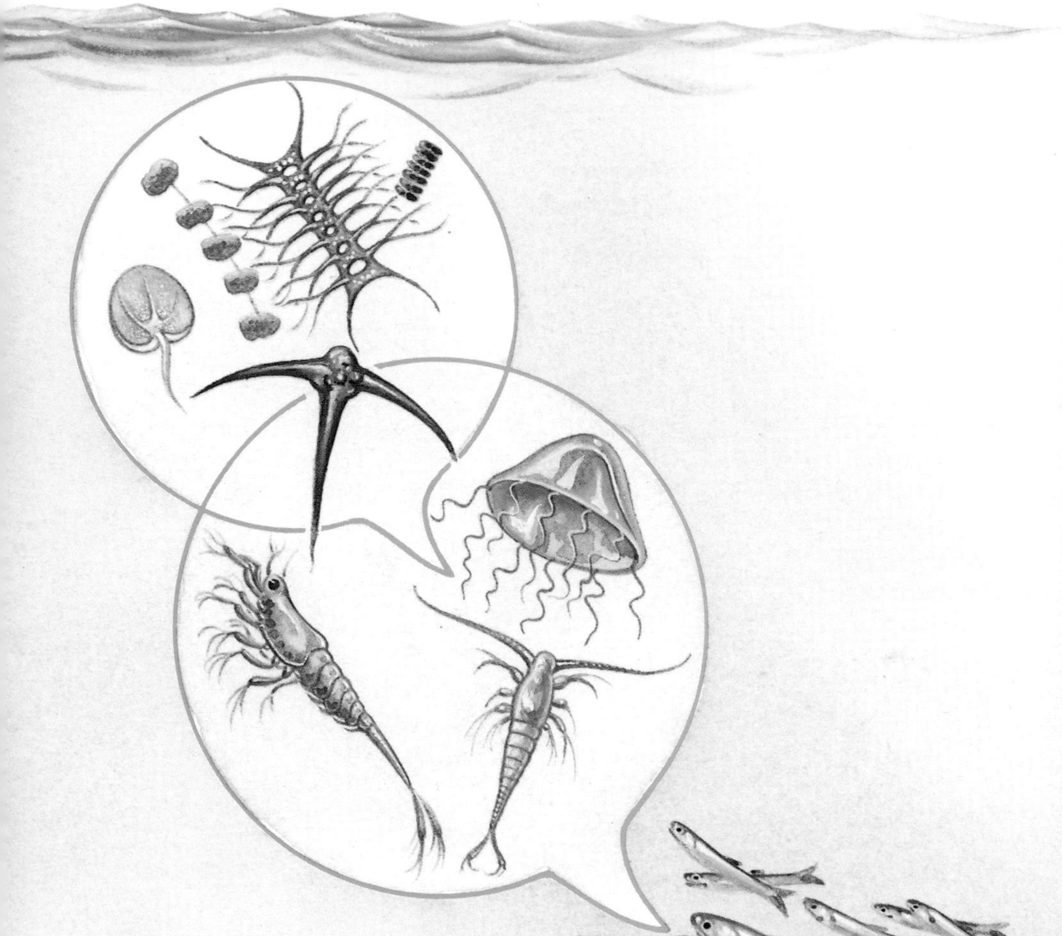

► *The pathway of just one sort of ocean food chain is illustrated here. Plant plankton grows with the help of the Sun – and is fed on by animal plankton. These small animals are caught in the millions by plankton-eating fish such as the school of anchovies. Fish like herring and pilchards feed in just the same way. Other larger fish, like cod and haddock, feed on the smaller fish, while the cod can be preyed on by single sharks.*

sunlight and use it in the process called photosynthesis to make new living material.

This Sun-powered production line is the starting point for almost every food chain in the sea. A food chain is a line of feeding links between one type of creature and another.

In the ocean's sunlit zones, plant plankton grow and multiply. These tiny plant particles are devoured by small animal plankton creatures like fish fry. Fish and squid eat these small fry, but are eaten, in turn, by yet larger fish. And so it goes on until there is a top predator like a great white shark, which can be killed only by humans, old age, or disease.

A food chain need not be long. It is shortest when a huge sea animal feeds directly on plankton. Some of the biggest ocean animals feed this way – basking sharks, and baleen whales like the blue whale.

◀ *Puffins are birds that swim underwater to catch fish such as the sand eels shown here.*

Puffins nest on land in old, empty rabbit burrows.

A walrus senses the location of its food on the sea bottom using its flat snout covered with sensitive bristles. It then grubs food up with its tusks of ivory.

The octopus has a powerful beak which can pierce or crush crab and lobster shells.

Gannets are large seabirds that plunge into the ocean from the air to catch fish.

▶ *These delicate blue creatures are sea squirts that strain tiny food particles from seawater. They do this by pulling the water in through a mouth opening. After the water has gone through a filter bag which holds back the food, it is then pushed out through a second hole.*

NEW LIFE IN THE SEA

To leave behind survivors when they themselves die, all sea creatures must be able to make copies of themselves – produce young. This multiplication happens in many ways. Some sea anemones, corals, jellyfish, and sea squirts can make new animals in a very simple way. A new baby version grows from a bud on the side of the adult animal. When it is ready, this bud breaks off to start a separate life.

Most sea animals, though, work in couples – a male or "father" and a female or "mother." The male makes sperm which join up with eggs from the female. After this joining, or fertilization, a new animal grows and develops.

For most sea animals, the chances of any single egg managing to survive all the dangers of the sea, and grow up to become an adult, are very, very slight. To balance this problem, most ocean animals produce large numbers of eggs so that at least some will grow up. A single female cod can lay four million eggs in one year.

FACT FILE

Male octopuses do not have a penis. They pass a packet of sperm into the female's body with the special spoon-shaped end of one of their tentacles.

Grenadier fish males make loud noises in the breeding season to attract their mates. They do this by vibrating their gas-filled swim bladders.

Male cardinal fish keep fertilized eggs in their mouths for several days for protection.

California fish called grunion come at night in huge schools to the sea's edge to mate and lay their eggs. The mating fish half bury themselves in the wet sand. When the eggs are laid they are protected by the sand.

▼ *A female flounder lays thousands of small eggs at one time. In most fish, the fertilization of eggs takes place outside the mother's body in the sea. The male sheds his sperm over the eggs as they are laid so they are fertilized.*

▶ *Many of the small animals in the plankton are young sea animals. These are shrimp larvae.*

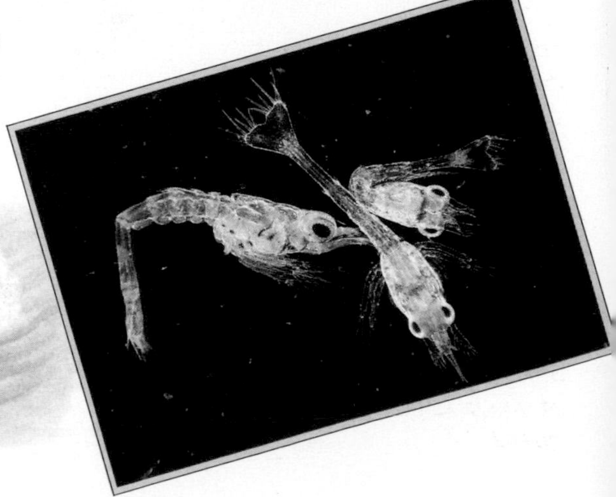

► *The males of the strange-shaped fish called seahorses protect fertilized eggs in a pouch. This one is giving birth to the young that grow from the eggs.*

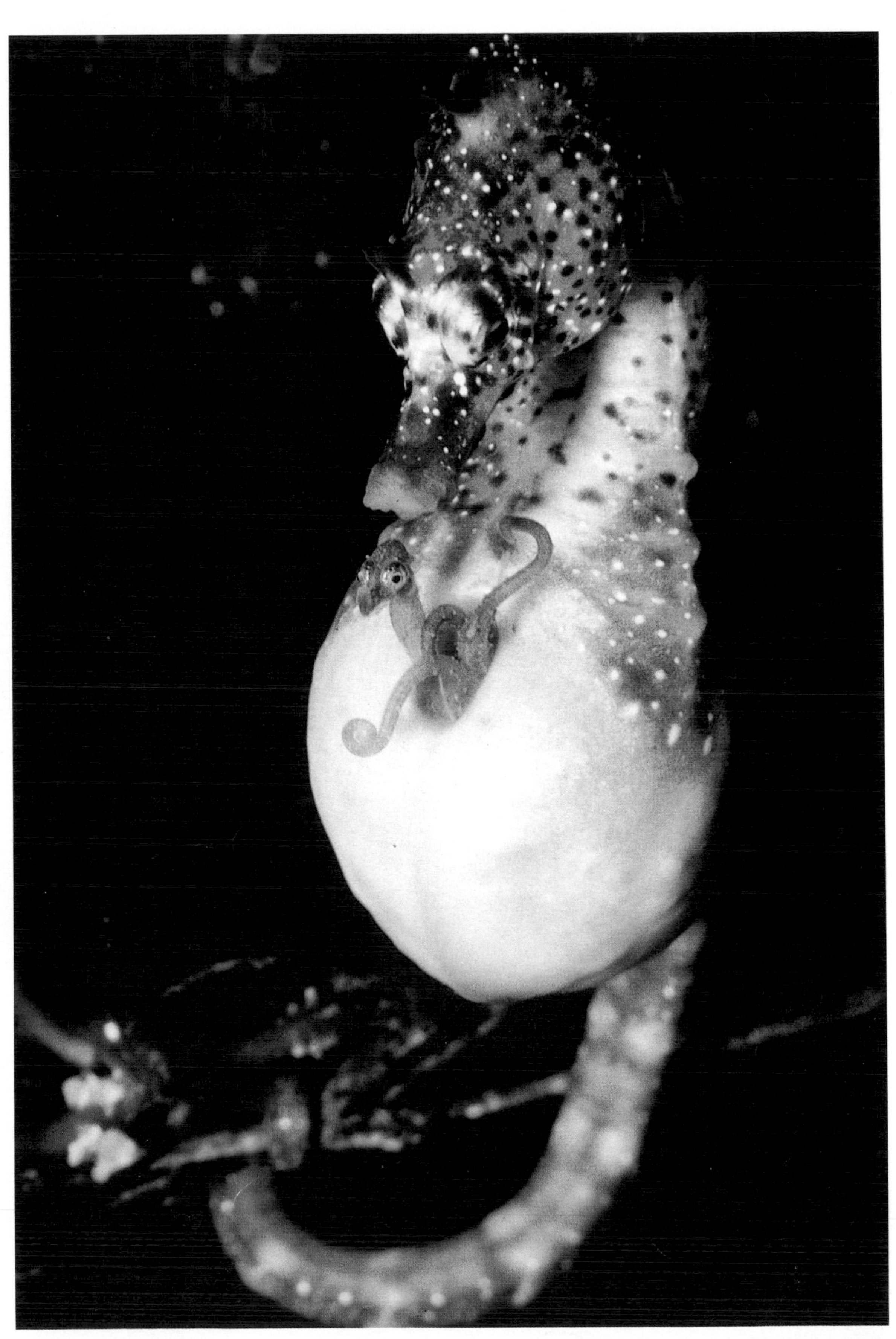

▲ *The female octopus lays thousands of eggs in clusters like grapes in a cave or hole. She then guards them for more than two months until they hatch safely. She does not feed herself at all while on guard.*

MARINE MIGRATIONS

Every large area of land or continent on our planet is separated from the others by water. But every sea is joined to every other part of the world's seas and oceans.

This ocean link-up gives some sea animals the opportunity to move anywhere in the world. Many of them do so and often cover vast distances. To make their migrations, they need stamina and skillful navigation.

Seabirds, such as terns and shearwaters, make huge journeys over water to feeding grounds and nesting sites. In the water itself, sharks, whales, turtles, and many fish also make very long migration journeys. We can often only guess how they travel thousands of miles in the correct direction. Perhaps they can taste changes in different currents, or make out the shape of the sea bottom with an electrical sense.

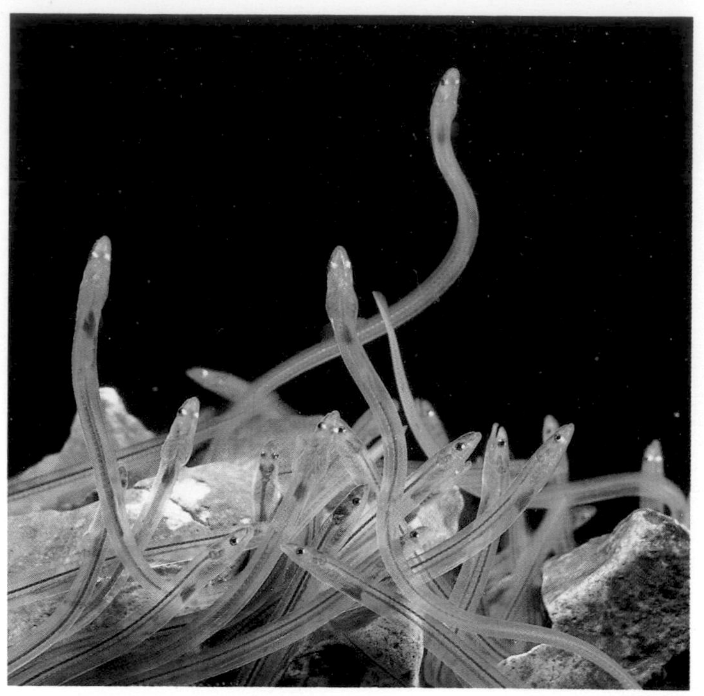

◀ *These baby eels, or elvers, are already three or four years old when they swim into European rivers. The eels take another 10 years to grow up. They then change color, grow bigger eyes, and migrate all the way back to breed in the Sargasso Sea where they were born.*

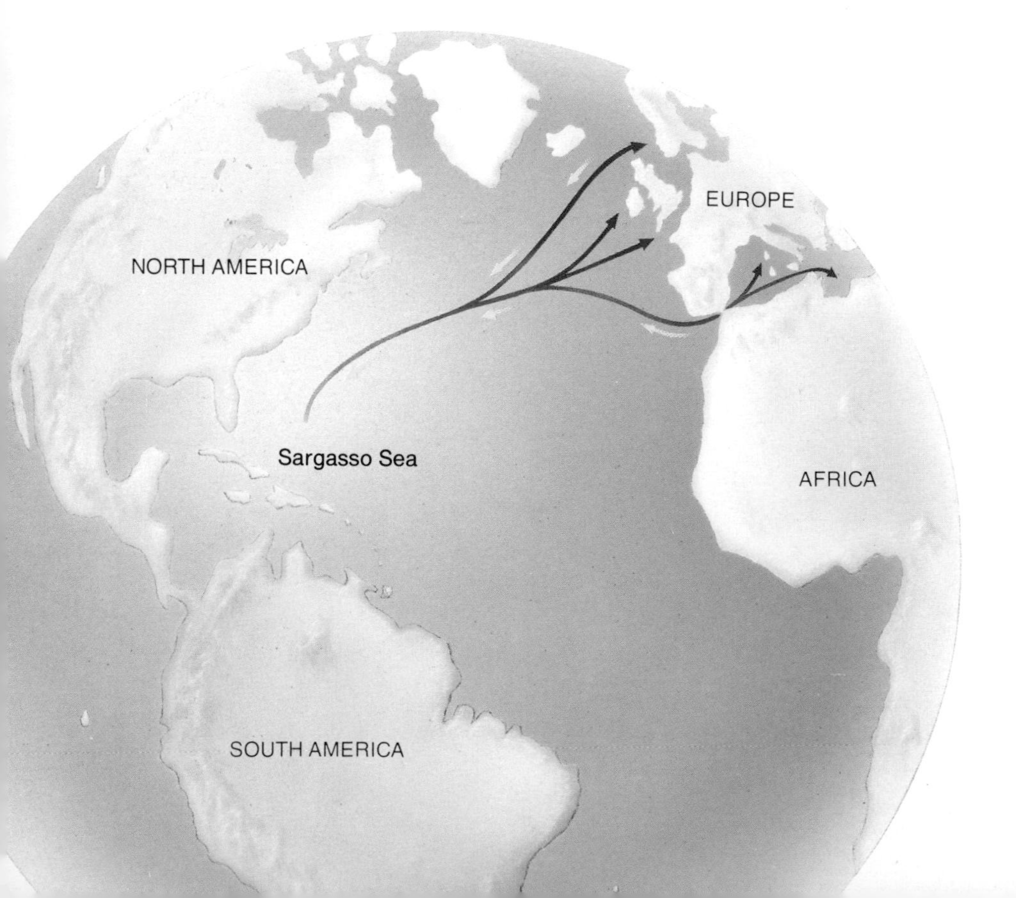

▼ *Eels breed in the Sargasso Sea off the southeast coast of North America. Their tiny larvae then take about three years to float as plankton across the Atlantic. Several years later they return.*

FACT FILE

Migrating salmon in the open ocean probably steer by the Sun and stars. Once near the coast, they use a sense of underwater "smell" to find the river up which they will swim to lay their eggs.

Humpback whales feed in the cold waters of the Arctic Ocean, but migrate back to the warmer waters of Hawaii where their young are born.

Arctic terns, graceful gull-like seabirds, hold the long-distance migration record. Every year, the birds fly from nesting sites in the Arctic to the waters of the Antarctic and back. This is a round trip of some 22,370 miles (36,000 km).

Each clutch laid by a female green turtle will contain about a hundred white leathery eggs. Only one will survive, if it is lucky.

AFRICA

Ascension Island

Brazil

SOUTH AMERICA

▲ *Green turtles feed on underwater plants off the coast of Brazil. They breed, though, on Ascension Island, a tiny outcrop of rock which is about 870 miles (1,400 km) away.*

◀ *Once hatched, the young turtles migrate to feed off the Brazilian coast like their parents. They return to Ascension two years later to breed on the same beaches.*

BORN ON THE BEACH

The female turtle scrapes a deep hole with her back flippers and deposits her eggs. She then fills it in and carefully hides all trace of the hole by smoothing the sand. In the warm sand, young turtles in the eggs soon grow, hatch out, and scuttle back to the sea.

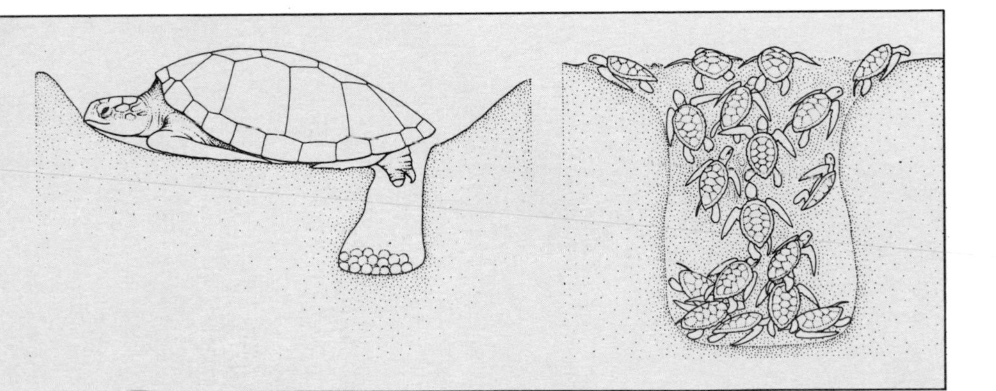

SHARKS – KILLERS OF THE DEEP

More than 340 different types of sharks live in the seas of the world. Not all of them are frightening, sharp-toothed hunters, although the shark family does include some of the fiercest flesh eaters in the sea.

Some of them, like the great white shark, the tiger shark, and the bull shark, are definitely known to have killed human beings. Many feed on other fish, and some just scoop shellfish and other small prey off the sea bottom.

Sharks belong to a primitive group of fish. Like their close relatives, the flat skates and rays, rat fish and rabbit fish, they all have skeletons made of gristle (cartilage) instead of bone. Most sharks have five gill slits on each side of the head, which take oxygen from the water. Often the top lobe of the tail fin is bigger than the lower one.

There are other differences between sharks and ordinary fish. Sharks do not, for instance, have a gas-filled swim bladder like other fish for controlling their buoyancy in the water. But although they are heavier than seawater, they do not sink because they keep swimming all the time.

Moving forward makes their large pectoral fins produce "lift" to keep them up just like a plane's wings do in flight.

Sharks' mouths are filled with many rows of teeth. The ones at the front of each row are the ones actually in use. When they wear out, the ones just behind them move forward and take their place. A shark may have as many as 24,000 teeth in its lifetime.

The skin of a shark is incredibly tough and rough; it feels like coarse sandpaper. This is caused by a covering of thousands of tiny skin scales, called denticles, each built like a tiny enamel-covered tooth.

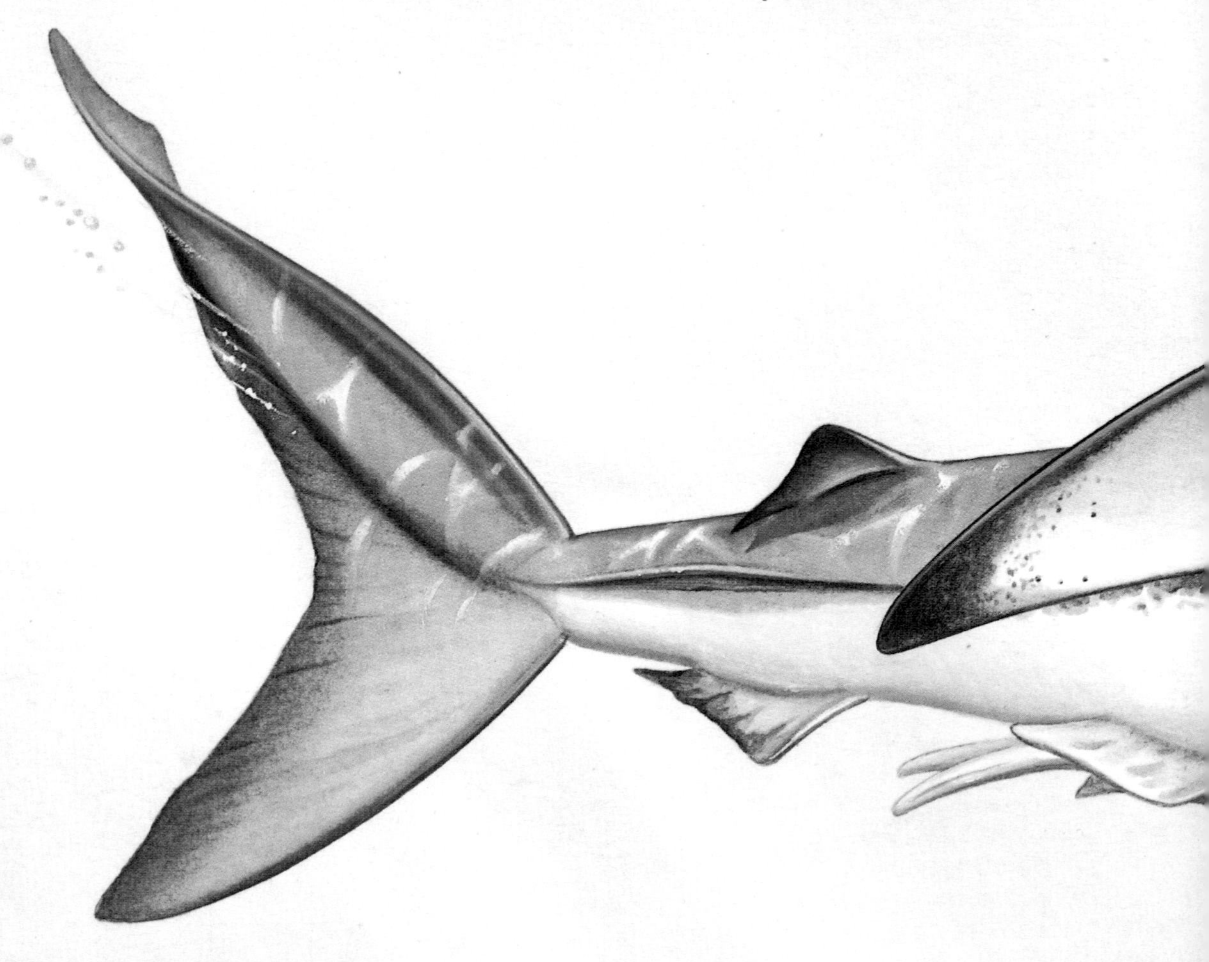

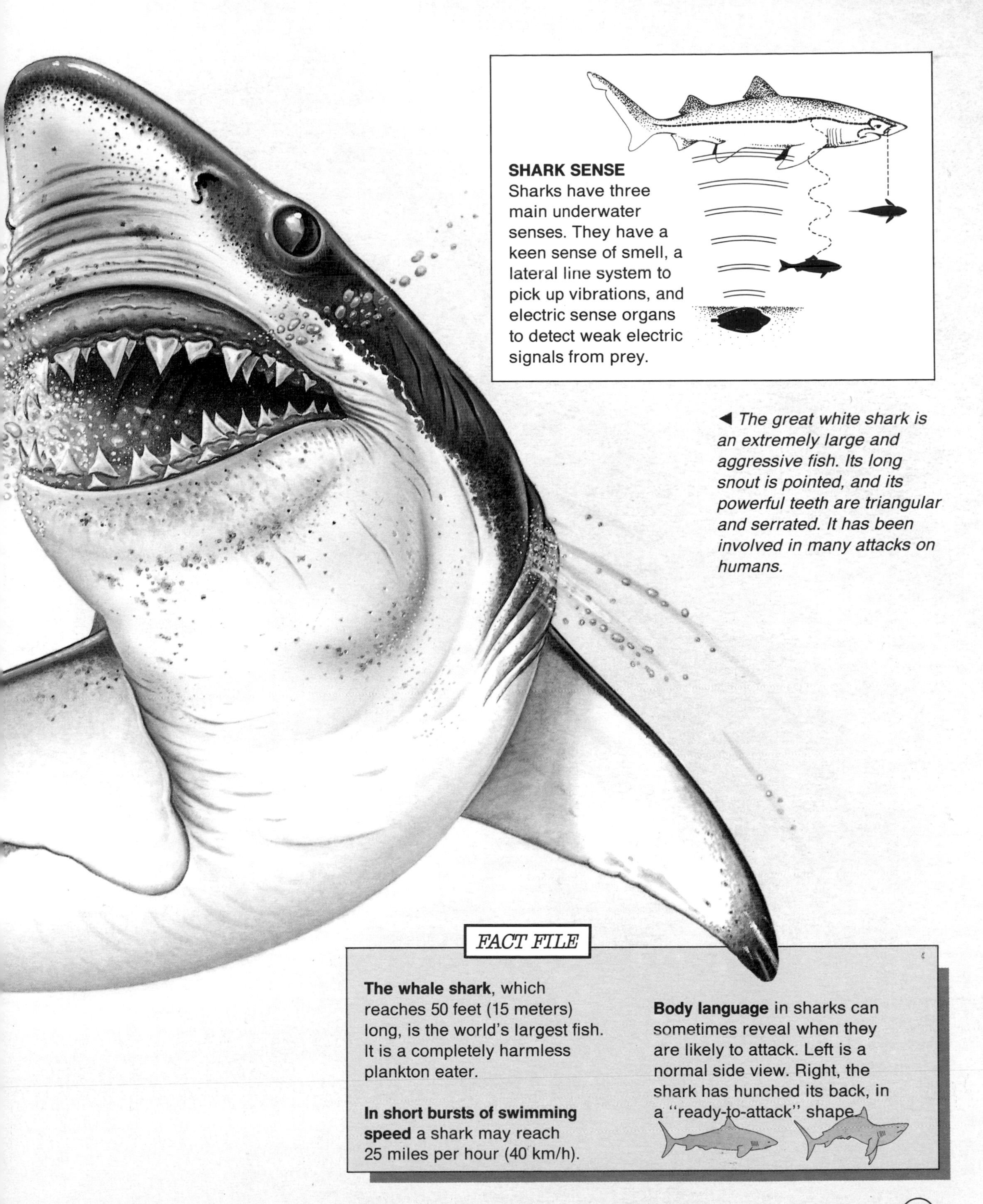

SHARK SENSE
Sharks have three main underwater senses. They have a keen sense of smell, a lateral line system to pick up vibrations, and electric sense organs to detect weak electric signals from prey.

◀ The great white shark is an extremely large and aggressive fish. Its long snout is pointed, and its powerful teeth are triangular and serrated. It has been involved in many attacks on humans.

FACT FILE

The whale shark, which reaches 50 feet (15 meters) long, is the world's largest fish. It is a completely harmless plankton eater.

In short bursts of swimming speed a shark may reach 25 miles per hour (40 km/h).

Body language in sharks can sometimes reveal when they are likely to attack. Left is a normal side view. Right, the shark has hunched its back, in a "ready-to-attack" shape.

SHARKS – DESIGNS FOR DEATH

The classic shark body design is the one seen in the famous movie, *Jaws.* The great white shark in the film had the typical shark shape – streamlined, large fins including the dreaded top fin, a pointed snout, and a huge underslung mouth filled with rows of jagged teeth.

Sharks also come in other shapes and sizes. There are huge, blunt-nosed forms, like the basking shark, with hardly any teeth worth the name. They use their gills to strain plankton out of the water. There are flattened, bottom-dwelling carpet sharks, like the wobbegong; sawsharks with a toothed "saw" at the front of their head; and hammerheads with strange sideways-pointing head lobes that carry their eyes. Each shark design enables that species to catch its prey.

FACT FILE

Australia is the worst place in the world for shark attacks on people. There have been more than 300 proven cases of attacks.

The largest type of man-eating shark is the great white. The largest one ever caught was almost 30 feet (9 meters) long and probably weighed around 10,000 pounds (4,500 kg). It was captured off the Azores in 1978.

Sharks' bodies are very flexible, and their jaws can be pushed outward so that they can attack from any angle.

Not all sharks live in the sea. Bull sharks can be found hundreds of miles from the sea up large rivers like the Amazon. Bull sharks are greatly feared in the Ganges in India, where they attack pilgrims washing in the river.

Cookiecutter sharks use a circle of razor-sharp teeth to gouge flesh out of the sides of dolphins and whales.

Of about 344 known shark species, only 27 are known to have attacked people or boats.

► *The great white shark is actually a dirty gray color. It has large, triangular, jagged teeth which it uses to kill fish – including other sharks – seals, turtles, and dolphins. It has killed more people than any other shark species. Great whites are found in all the major oceans of the world.*

► *Whitetip reef sharks live around coral caves in reefs and lagoons. This whitetip is carrying a remora on its body. These unusual fish have a large, ribbed suction pad on top of their head that enables them to ride hanging on to a shark.*

◄ *Hammerhead sharks have the most unusual shark body shape. The sides of their head are stretched out sideways into two flattened flaps. At the end of each one is an eye and a nostril. Some scientists think that it gives the sharks a super-sensitive "stereo" power of smell so that prey can be easily found.*

WHALES – THE LARGEST SEA CREATURES

More than 65 million years ago, a group of flesh-eating mammals left the land to live in the sea. Over millions more years, they lost their back legs, grew flippers instead of front legs, and developed flattened tails for swimming. Their noses moved from their snout to the top of their head and became an air-breathing blowhole, and they got rid of all their hair except for a few bristles on the snout. The whales had arrived.

There are now 76 species of whales, dolphins, and porpoises swimming in the seas of the world. They range from the 4-feet (1.2 meter) long common porpoise to the stupendous blue whale. This whale, which can grow to 120 feet (36 meters) long, is the largest animal of any kind in the world today. It is more than that – it is the largest animal that has *ever* lived.

The whales – and their dolphin and porpoise relatives – have made the most complete change to a watery life of any of the air-breathing animals. Although, like all other mammals, they still breathe air and give birth to live young which are suckled with milk, in almost every other way they look like fish.

Ever since people have gone to sea in boats, these huge animals have been killed for food and for the thick layer of fat, or blubber, that is found under their skin. Modern whaling methods have been so successful that many of the large whales face extinction. Now almost all commercial whaling is illegal.

FACT FILE

The blubber of a large blue whale can be up to 10 inches (25 cm) thick.

The stomach of a humpback whale can hold as much as 1,300 pounds (590 kg) of krill food. Krill are small shrimp in the animal plankton.

The outsides of many large whales are covered with huge barnacles, seaweed, and pink whale lice.

Toothed whales can usually navigate underwater and find their prey in the dark using a type of sonar system.

Whalebone, the hairy plates in the mouth of filter-feeding whales, was once used for making corsets.

▼ *Some filter-feeding whales use a bubble fence when catching their shrimpy diet. They release air in a ring of bubbles that seems to drive the krill into one area. The whale then rises in the center of the bubble ring, trapping the krill in its huge mouth.*

▲ *This gray whale shows the whalebone filter in its mouth which is used to catch krill.*

The whalebone is not bone at all, but a tough and stringy sort of hardened hair material.

◀ *These two enormous sea creatures are examples of the two main groups of large whales. The killer whale, a toothed underwater killer, is black and white. Behind is a minke whale, which strains animal plankton from the water using a filter in its mouth made of baleen.*

WHALES – THE GENTLE GIANTS

It is easy to imagine that all whales are alike and that they simply come in a variety of different sizes. In fact, in body shape, behavior, and the ways that they gather their food, these air-breathing underwater giants show a range of differences.

There are small dolphins that do not live in the sea at all. They are the river dolphins and can be found in the Amazon and in the rivers of India and China.

There are the sea-going porpoises and dolphins. The main difference between these two groups of small whales with teeth is that porpoises have blunt front ends. Many of the more common dolphins have pointed "beaks." Larger whales with teeth include the killer whale and the sperm whale.

The most specialized whales do not have teeth at all. The whalebone, or baleen, whales trap huge volumes of water in their mouths, then push the water out through their whalebone "whiskers" by pushing their tongue up like a piston to the roof of their mouth. The water is pushed out, but the krill remains behind as food.

FACT FILE

A narwhal is a whale with a tusk. The males of this Arctic species have a single tusk, up to 9 feet (3 meters) long, sticking forward from the mouth. It is a single, very long, twisted tooth.

The songs of the white whale caused it to be called the sea canary by nineteenth-century whalers.

The skin of all whales is very flexible. This means that it can change its shape in response to tiny pressure changes in the water. This lets it slip easily through the water.

Dolphins have large brains with very many folds in them. They can be taught very complicated tricks in oceanariums.

▲ *Although whales can stay underwater for up to an hour, they do have to come to the surface to breathe. Air is pushed out of the blowhole very rapidly, and a huge new breath is taken in through the same hole before the whale dives again.*

► *A humpback whale leaping from the water.*

▲ *This common dolphin likes to swim around fast-moving ships, sometimes "surf riding" on the ship's bow wave.*

▲ Killer whales are large, toothed whales that feed on fish, squid, sea lions, and other whales.

◀ This close view of a blue whale makes it clear that a blowhole is a very special nose. Inside, it is divided into two giant "nostrils."

THE WATER CYCLE

It was a mystery to ancient peoples why the level of the sea stayed the same from year to year, when all the time, rain and rivers were pouring more and more water into it. Now we think we know what is happening. There is only a certain amount of water in the world which never changes. It is being used over and over again in what is called a water cycle.

The Sun shines on the oceans and warms them. Much of the water at the surface turns into water vapor, a sort of cool, invisible steam, which rises into the air. High above the Earth, it is cold enough for the vapor to cool into tiny water droplets that float around in the sky in huge groups – we call them clouds.

If anything makes the clouds cool down the droplets join up to form drops large enough to fall to the ground. Depending on the temperature, they fall as rain or snow. The water that falls forms streams and rivers or goes into the ground. Most of it finally runs back into the sea where it can be heated by the Sun and turned into clouds and the cycle begins again.

Clouds, rain, and snow are made of pure, fresh water. As this water runs over rocks, through the soil, or along rivers, it picks up small amounts of chemicals (salts and minerals) from the rocks. Like sugar in a cup of coffee, these chemicals dissolve and are carried by the rivers to the sea. Over billions of years, this one-way movement of chemicals has made the sea salty. The salts of the sea all originally came from the land.

FACT FILE

97 percent of the world's water is in the oceans; 2 percent is frozen in glaciers and the ice caps; while only 1 percent is the freshwater found in rivers, lakes, and underground.

The Pacific Ocean is the largest collection of water in the world. It is as big as all the other oceans and seas put together.

Seawater salts contain precious metals like gold and uranium. There is even enough magnesium in seawater for it to be used to make alloys.

If the Earth's climate is warmed up too much, by the "greenhouse effect," the ice in the ice caps would melt. This would make the sea level rise –

▲ *These are shallow, saltwater lakes, close to the sea in Portugal, called salt pans. Water is let into them and the strong Sun evaporates all the water and leaves the salt behind as white crystals. These are then used for eating and cooking.*

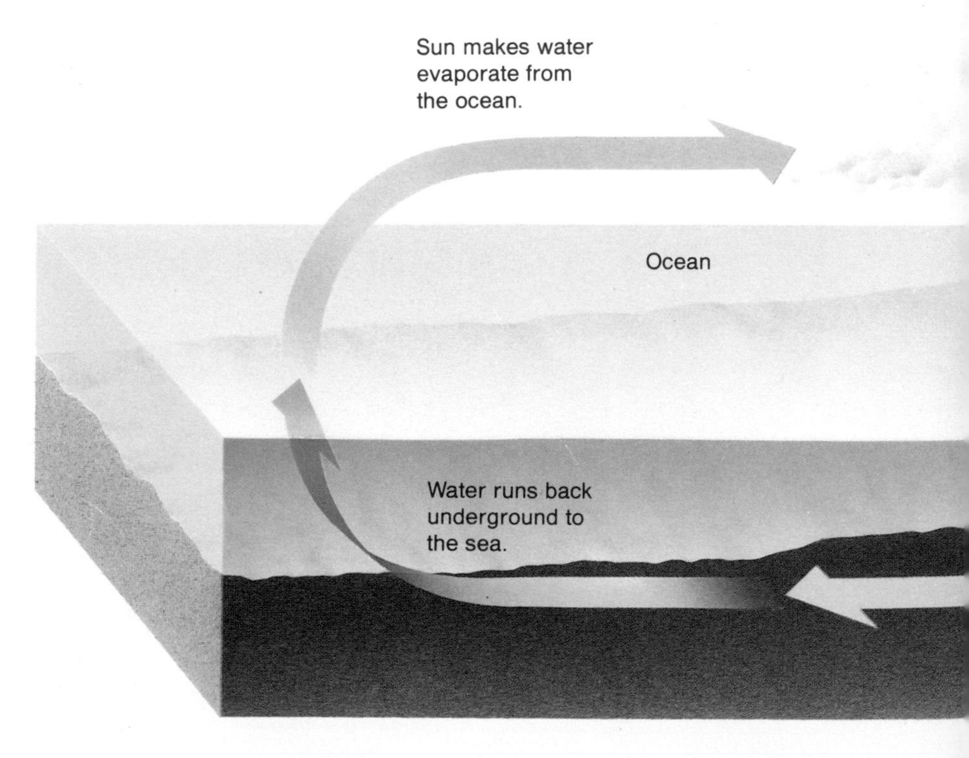

completely flooding some low-lying countries.

The sea is full of salt. Even in an average-sized seawater swimming pool, there are $3\frac{1}{2}$ tons of salt. This is the same weight as 100 average-sized 11-year-old girls!

► *This amazing picture was taken by the astronauts on* Apollo 16 *while they were making their journey to the Moon and back in 1972. The picture shows clearly the huge amount of water in the world – in this case, in the oceans around North America.*

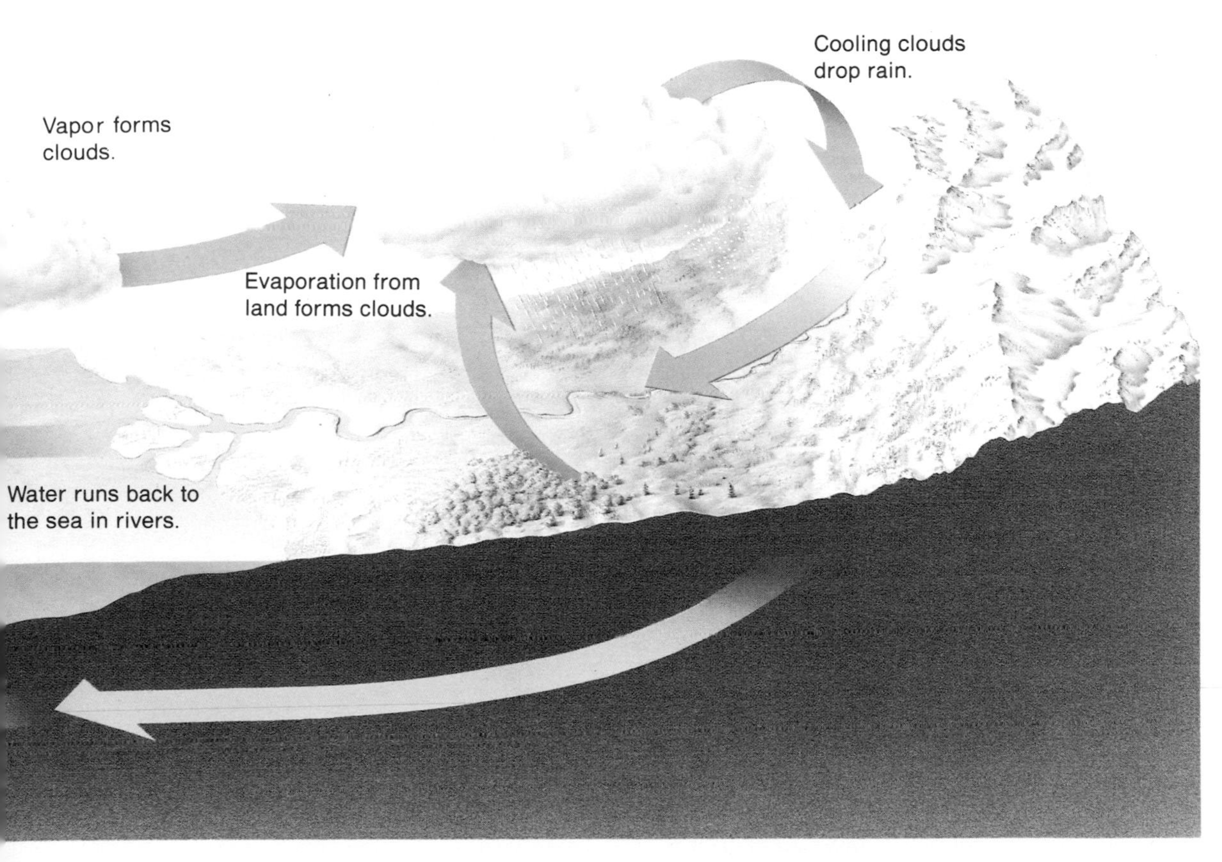

◄ *This diagram shows the main parts of the ocean's water cycle. The Sun evaporates seawater, making water vapor that turns into clouds.*

As the clouds move higher and pass over mountains, they cool and drop their water as rain or snow. Carried by rivers, or by seeping through the ground, most of this water returns to the sea to start the cycle all over again.

THE OCEAN'S TIDES

On vacation, you may go to a sandy beach for a day's outing. When you arrive in the morning, you sit close to the water's edge so that you can get in to swim easily. By the middle of the afternoon, the tide has gone out – you have to walk quite a long way over the sand to go for a swim. Where does the water go when the tide goes out?

The tides are an amazing fact that we all take for granted. When the tide goes out, the water does not disappear – it just moves from one place to another on the Earth's surface. This happens because the ocean's waters are pulled toward the Moon by gravity.

Gravity is the force that makes objects fall to the ground when you drop them – the Earth's gravity pulls the objects toward it. In the same way, the Moon's gravity pulls the oceans toward the Moon. The part of the oceans directly under the Moon are heaped up into a bulge of water. There is a similar bulge on the opposite side of the Earth as well. In between the bulging areas, the water levels are lower.

If you are sitting on a beach in a "bulge" place, you will see a high tide there. If you are where the levels are lower, you will see a low tide.

Because the Earth spins around once every 24 hours – that is why we have days and nights – each spot on the Earth's surface is under the Moon about once every 24 hours. This means that in one spin – one night plus one day – you would pass through two water bulges and two lower levels, that is two high tides and two low tides.

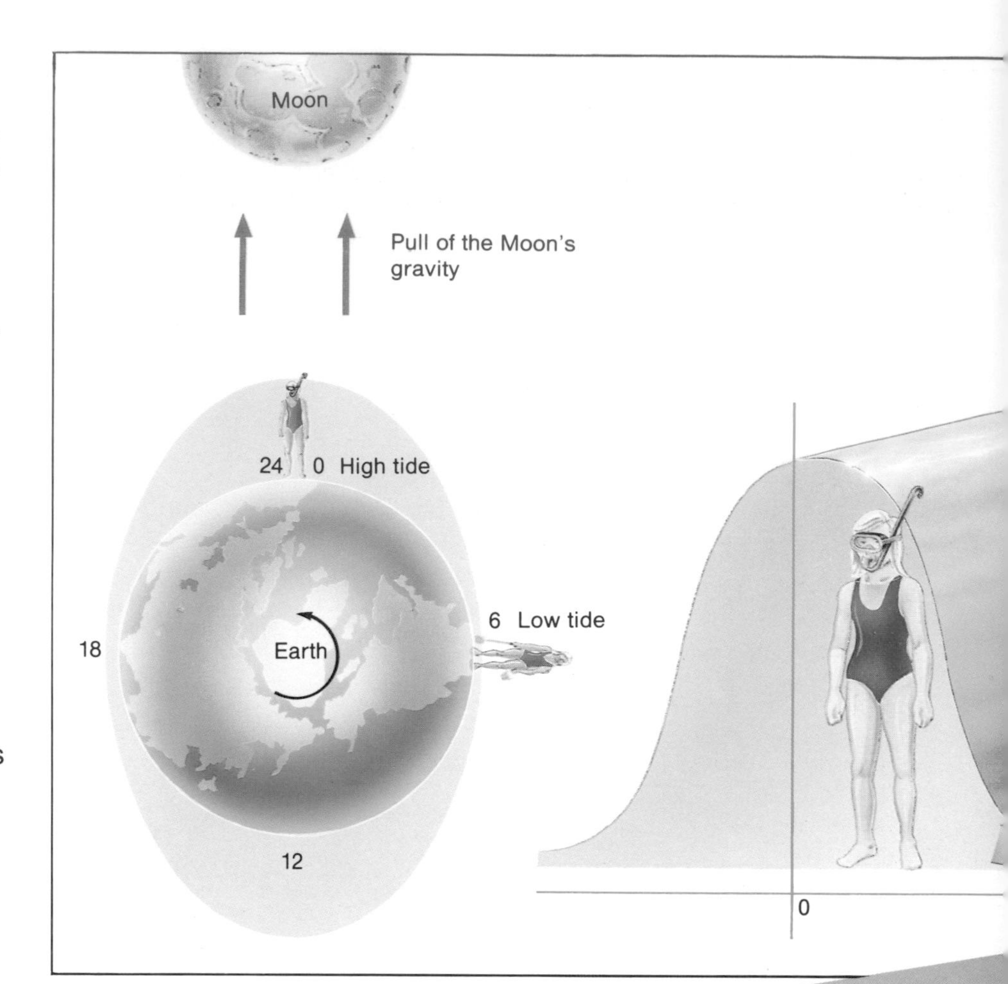

These diagrams show why there are two high tides and two low tides every 24 hours. On the left, a picture of the spinning Earth shows the ocean bulges caused by the pull of the Moon's gravity. On the right is shown what happens to the sea level on one beach as the Earth's spin takes that beach through two water bulges (high tides) and two lower levels (low tides) in one day and one night.

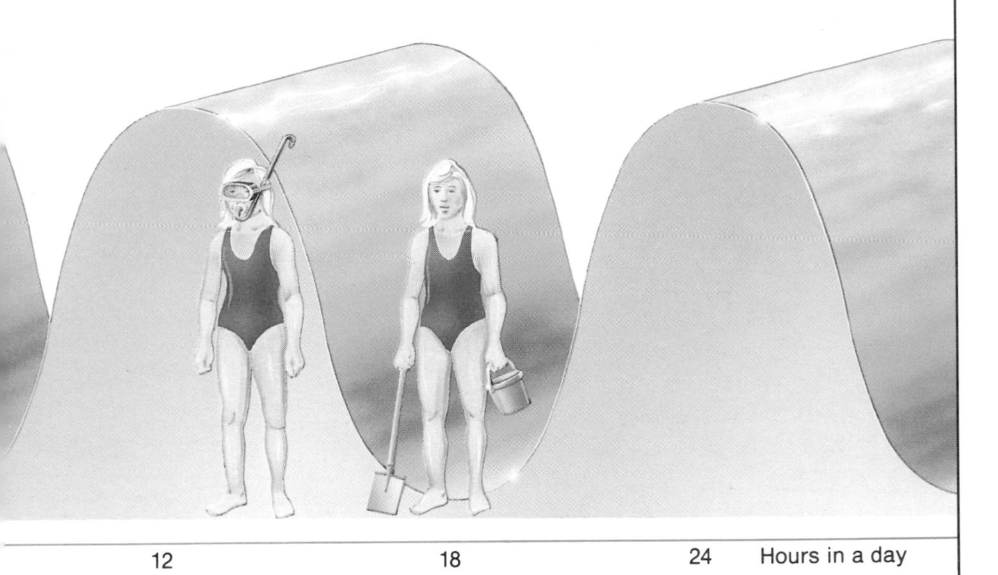

FACT FILE

The tides change with a monthly cycle. This is because the Moon orbits the Earth once every 28 days or so.

Spring tides are the times when the high tides are higher and the low ones lower than usual. **Neap tides** are times when the highs and lows are less extreme.

The phases of the Moon are linked with the tides. Spring tides come when the Moon is full; neaps happen when there is a half crescent Moon.

Tide power can be used by harnessing the movements of the sea. In the past, tide mills used the tidal flow to drive waterwheels in mills for grinding corn. Today, the falling and rising water can be used to provide electricity.

◀ *Tides are highest and lowest on coasts that face large oceans. Here are two pictures taken at such a place, the inlet at Portquin in Cornwall, England. It is strange to think that it is the Moon – a quarter of a million miles away from Cornwall – that makes the seawater move up and down like this.*

HURRICANE!

Hurricanes are the most powerful weather systems on Earth. They are huge, spiraling tropical storms that can be 500 miles (805 kilometers) across. They are only born over warm, tropical oceans, and they are given different names in different parts of the world.

The hurricanes in the North Atlantic start as ordinary tropical storms out in the middle of the ocean. But if the water under them is warm enough, a terrible change can come over the storm. The warm sea makes more and more seawater evaporate, and this extra water vapor adds fuel to the storm. The fuel speeds it up and makes it bigger. When the spiraling winds reach a continuous 74 miles per hour (119 kilometers per hour) or more, the tropical storm has officially become a hurricane.

Winds push the spinning hurricane westward toward the islands of the Caribbean and the east coast of the United States or Mexico. Once the hurricane meets the land and releases its energy as waves, wind, and rain, it dies out. These natural forces can cause devastation to coasts and low-lying islands.

FACT FILE

Naming a hurricane. As hurricanes form each year, they are given an individual name. Each name moves on to start with the next letter of the alphabet, and boys' and girls' names alternate.

6,000 people died in 1900 when a hurricane hit Galveston Island in Texas.

In 1965, Hurricane Betsy caused havoc in southern Florida and Louisiana. As many as 75 people were killed and $1,400,000,000 worth of damage was caused.

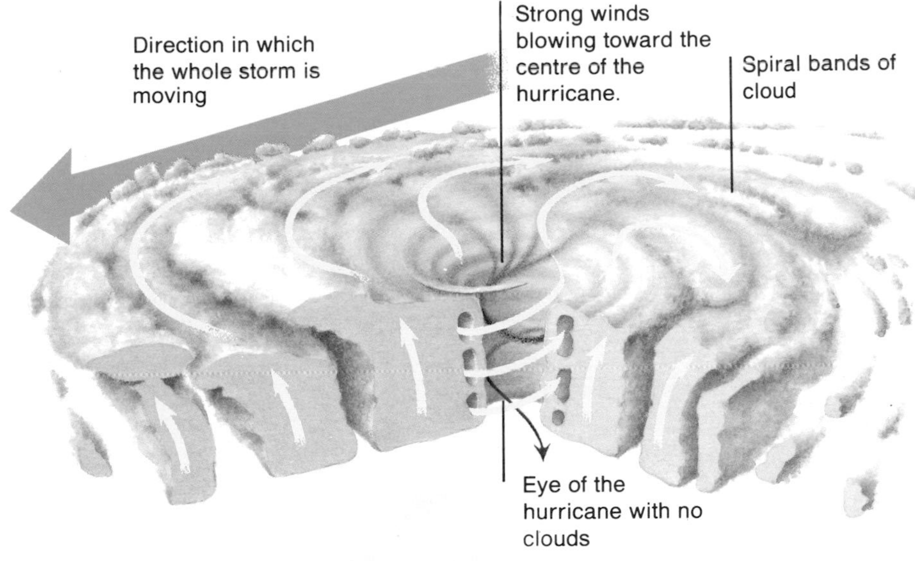

◀ These immense storm waves were battering the coast of the Caribbean island of Martinique in 1979. They were caused by Hurricane David.

▼ Cameras on weather satellites and in spacecraft let scientists track the path and speed of hurricanes.

▲ This cutaway picture of a hurricane shows the spiraling winds of the storm, which look like water swirling down a bathtub drain. The swirling, though, is going on at more than 100 mph (160 km/h)! The cloudless "eye" in the middle of the storm can be seen with a wall of clouds all around it.

When the "eye" in the middle of a hurricane passes you, for a short while the winds, which had speeds of more than 100 mph (160 km/h), drop to nothing and the sky clears.

Hurricane Gilbert set a record in 1988. It caused steady winds of 170 mph (273 km/h) and gusts of more than 200 mph (322 km/h) while it devastated Jamaica.

A hurricane happens in the North Atlantic. In the Pacific it is called a typhoon, in the Indian Ocean and around Australia it is called a tropical cyclone.

THE POWER OF THE WAVES

The surface of the seas and oceans is never flat. As wind speeds get faster, the tiny ripples on the water, which are always present – even in still weather – begin to grow into waves. Some of the great energy of the wind is turned into wave motion in the surface layers of the seawater.

The waves move in ups and downs – the ups, or rises, are called crests, the downs, or falls, are called troughs.

The height of a wave – from trough to crest – gets bigger as the wind gets stronger. Waves also get higher and higher the farther they are able to travel in one direction before they hit land. This is why there are never very big waves on lakes.

A wave approaching the shore and then breaking on it looks as though water is rolling toward the beach. This is not really the case. Until it breaks, the water in a wave is just going up and down in a circle in the same place. It is much the same as when you tie one end of a jump rope to a fence and wiggle the other end up and down. Waves pass along the rope from your hand to the fence, but the rope itself does not get nearer the fence – it is still in the same place it was before you started wiggling it. The sea waves are doing the same thing; the wave crests move toward the beach, but the water stays where it is.

When a wave ends its life, it breaks on the shore. When the bottom of the wave is slowed down by dragging along the shore bottom, its crest overtakes it and topples foward. The "breaker" shoots water up the beach or at a cliff and can cause it to wear away.

► *Sand and rocks thrown at the shore by the waves can cut away soft or even hard rock. Here on the Dorset coast of southern England is a natural sea arch called Durdle Dor.*

► *This shows the movements of water in waves approaching a sandy shore. The movement of the water changes as it gets closer to the shore. Finally, the crest of the wave tips forward and breaks. The water shoots up the beach and then streams back before the next wave breaks.*

FACT FILE

When an Atlantic wave hits the shore, the pressure is the same as an elephant sitting on a small table.

Rocks weighing 110 pounds (50 kg) can be thrown more than 130 feet (40 meters) above the level of the sea by powerful storm waves.

"White horses" are waves out at sea whose tops have been broken into foam by strong, gusty winds.

Energy from the waves can be used to generate pollution-free electricity. The up-and-down motion of the waves can be used to work pumps or levers to run an electrical generator.

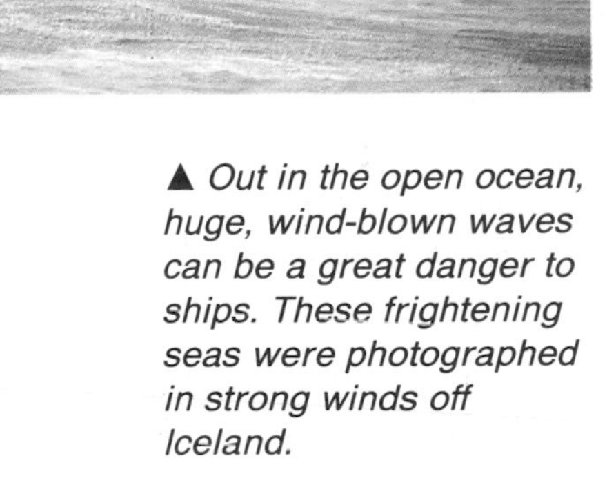

▲ *Out in the open ocean, huge, wind-blown waves can be a great danger to ships. These frightening seas were photographed in strong winds off Iceland.*

CORAL REEFS

A coral reef is the home of millions of tiny animals. Although it looks like a jumble of weird-shaped rocks, it is really the piled-up skeletons of coral animals, relatives of the sea anemone. During their life, soft-bodied coral animals, called polyps, make hard, limy skeletons around themselves. It is these which make up the reef.

The mass of the coral polyps live joined to one another in large colonies, so the rock skeletons they make can be very large. From holes in the skeleton, the feeding parts of the polyps can be pushed out like small sea anemones. They stun their food by using the stinging cells on their tentacles.

The coral animals must have warm seawater, so they are only found in tropical seas. To feed, they need clear unmuddied water, so they are not found near the ends of rivers where there is a lot of mud.

Corals do not live alone. Inside their bodies are plant cells. Because these need light, the corals have to live near the surface. This means that reefs are only made in shallow waters around land or islands, or in the tops of submerged islands.

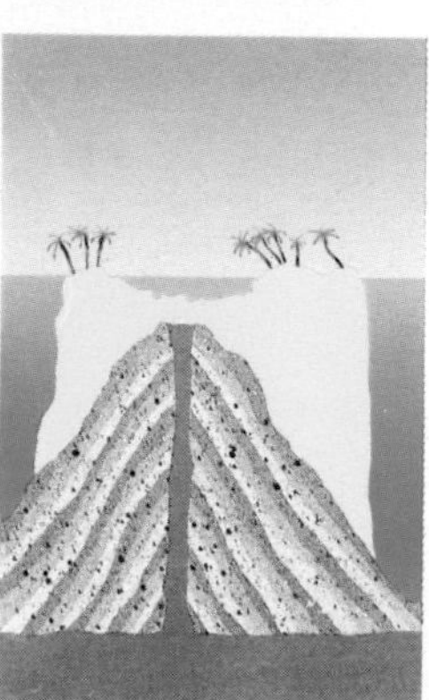

► *In warm seas, reefs can grow around volcanic islands as a fringe in shallow water. If the island slowly sinks, or the seas rise, the corals grow upward to stay in the light. This can, in the end, produce a ring-shaped island of coral. The ring is called an atoll.*

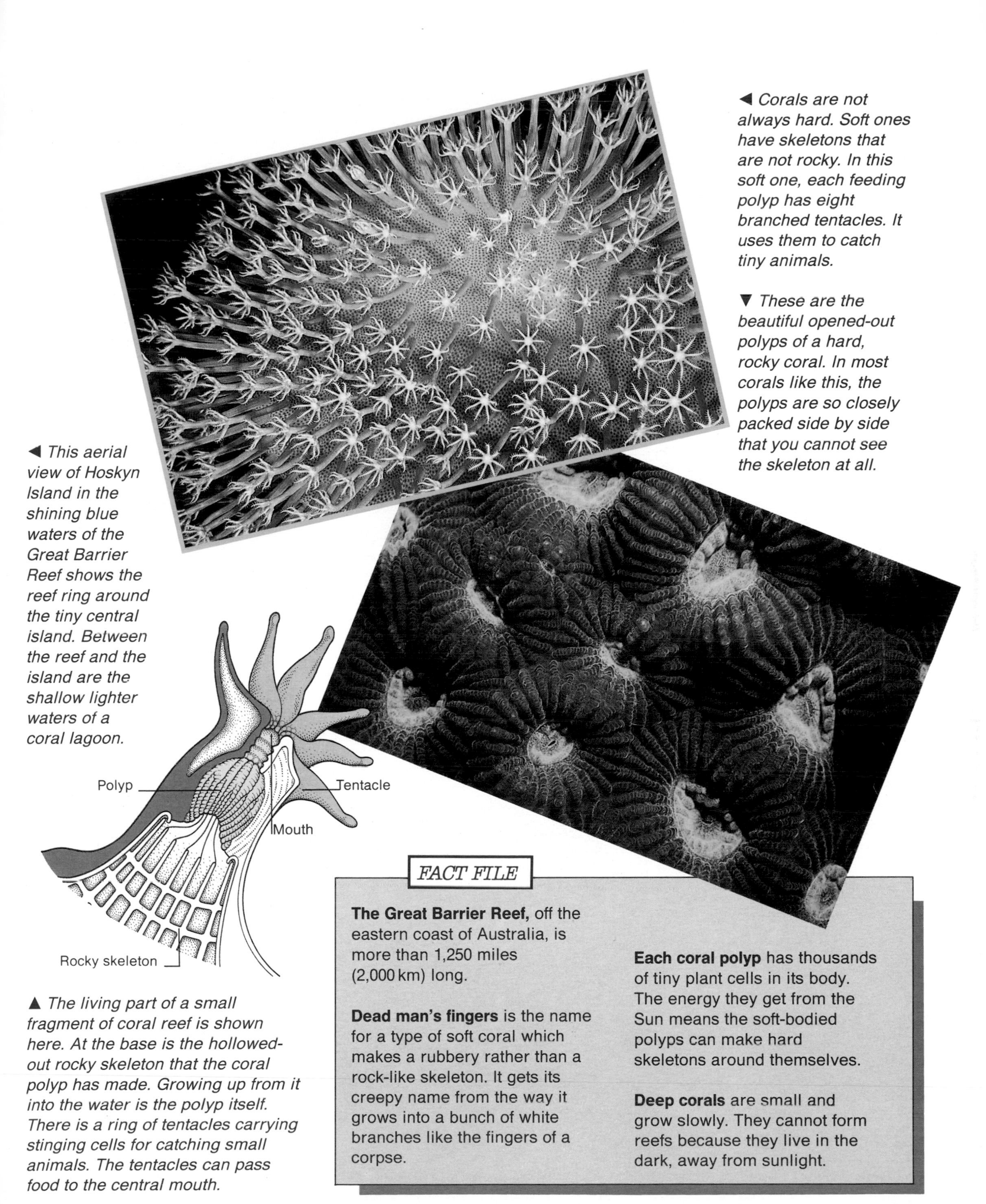

◀ *Corals are not always hard. Soft ones have skeletons that are not rocky. In this soft one, each feeding polyp has eight branched tentacles. It uses them to catch tiny animals.*

▼ *These are the beautiful opened-out polyps of a hard, rocky coral. In most corals like this, the polyps are so closely packed side by side that you cannot see the skeleton at all.*

◀ *This aerial view of Hoskyn Island in the shining blue waters of the Great Barrier Reef shows the reef ring around the tiny central island. Between the reef and the island are the shallow lighter waters of a coral lagoon.*

▲ *The living part of a small fragment of coral reef is shown here. At the base is the hollowed-out rocky skeleton that the coral polyp has made. Growing up from it into the water is the polyp itself. There is a ring of tentacles carrying stinging cells for catching small animals. The tentacles can pass food to the central mouth.*

FACT FILE

The Great Barrier Reef, off the eastern coast of Australia, is more than 1,250 miles (2,000 km) long.

Dead man's fingers is the name for a type of soft coral which makes a rubbery rather than a rock-like skeleton. It gets its creepy name from the way it grows into a bunch of white branches like the fingers of a corpse.

Each coral polyp has thousands of tiny plant cells in its body. The energy they get from the Sun means the soft-bodied polyps can make hard skeletons around themselves.

Deep corals are small and grow slowly. They cannot form reefs because they live in the dark, away from sunlight.

THE CORAL WORLD

The coral reef would be an amazing place even if it were only composed of the coral animals that built it. In fact, the coral reef itself provides an underwater landscape that is used as a home by a huge variety of other animals and plants.

The crevices and spaces in the twisting and turning shapes of the corals provide a never-ending supply of hiding places and protection for small animals. And large animals, like fish, live in the reef to feed on the smaller creatures.

Many of the fish that can be seen on a reef are brightly colored with bold markings. The reasons for this are not always understood. Some look like this as a warning of the fact that they are armed with poisonous spines or that they taste dreadful. This protects them from being eaten by other fish.

The showy displays of many others might be a way for males and females of the same species to recognize each other for mating. There might well be a greater need for this on reefs than in other undersea habitats because there are so many different species there.

▲ *A brain coral gets its name from its rounded shape and the grooves in its surface which make it look like a human brain.*

Moorish Idol

Striped-faced Unicornfish

Blue Tang

◀ *Gorgonians are fanlike, hard corals that spread out their rocky arms in a flat sheet across the flow of the water current. Polyps stretch out to catch food that flows past.*

▶ *Hard table corals stretch up from the reef on a single "leg." They do this so that their polyps are in a good water flow. In this way, food is carried to them.*

FACT FILE

Star wars! A crown of thorns starfish can kill coral polyps even when they are hidden deep inside their rocky skeleton. They release powerful juices that digest the polyps even while they hide.

Most corals work a night shift. In the daytime, the polyps sink down inside their rocky skeleton. They only stretch out to feed at sunset.

More sorts of animals are found in reefs than almost any other undersea habitat. The Great Barrier Reef has over 350 species of corals and almost 150 different sorts of sea urchins.

The female gall crab settles on a piece of coral and makes the coral grow around her. This keeps her safe, but unable to leave her coral prison.

CROWN OF THORNS STARFISH

This starfish feeds on corals and has recently become a serious pest – particularly on the Great Barrier Reef in Australia. These large starfish are not hurt by the stinging cells of the corals and are able to eat the coral polyps.

They do this by settling down on the surface of the coral and destroying whole patches of polyps. No one is sure what started this epidemic of starfish. In Australia, divers are now paid to kill them underwater to stop the damage they are causing.

DEEP SEA VENTS

In 1977 scientists on board the *Alvin* submersible mini-submarine were exploring in the near-freezing depths of the Galapagos Rift. This is a place in the Pacific Ocean where they knew that hot liquid lava was rising from inside the Earth onto the sea bottom to make new seabed rocks.

The scientists found the new rocks, but they also found a wonderland of extraordinary new creatures living in complete blackness there. These were the animals of the deep sea vents.

The vents are places on the seabed where seawater, heated by the molten rocks below, streams out of the sea floor into the freezing water above. In this warmed water lives a zoo of amazing animals. Giant red tube worms cling to the newly hardened lava. Basketball-sized clams cover the rocks, and blind white crabs scuttle over the clams. At this great depth there is no light, and crabs find their way by touch and taste.

None of these creatures lives anywhere other than the warm, cloudy waters of the vents. None lives on plant food. Instead, they all depend on bacteria which in darkness can live on the gas called hydrogen sulfide found in the vent water. This makes the animals of the deep sea vents unique in the world.

► *Like gigantic white kidney beans, these clams – covered with crabs – stick themselves to the new rock surfaces. Clams strain microbes from the warm vent seawater. Most of these microbes live by using chemicals dissolved in the water.*

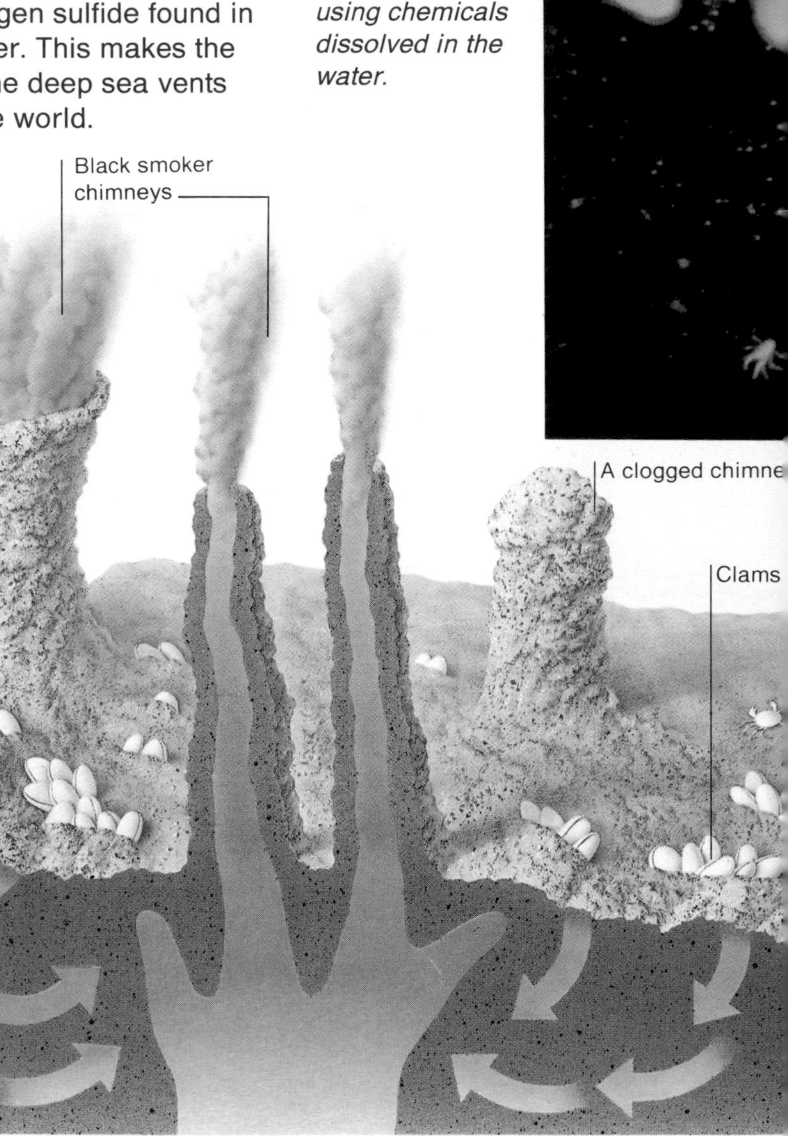

▲ *Seawater seeps through spongelike rocks on the seabed, coming close to the hot, liquid rock. In the rock, it picks up dissolved minerals and is also warmed.*

▲ *When the warmed water comes to the surface again, it shoots up as a hot, cloudy black stream from a chimney of solidified minerals. This is called a "black smoker."*

FACT FILE

The vent water often shoots out of chimneys at temperatures of 480°F/250°C. This would be superheated steam on land, but liquid water can be this hot under pressure on the seabed.

Vent clams can grow 1½ inches (4 cm) a year, which is 500 times faster than their seashore cousins. They grow this fast because of their rich food and the warm water they live in.

Where hot vent water mixes with normal, cold seawater, large mounds of minerals turn from liquid to solid and pile up on the seabed.

Solidifying lava or minerals eventually clog up all deep sea vents.

▲ *Tube worms up to 10 feet (3 meters) long are the strangest of all the vent animals. The bright-red front ends of the worms stick out of their protective white tubes. Despite their huge size, these worms have no mouth and no gut. They seem to get all their food from chemical-using bacteria that live deep inside their bodies as partners.*

◀ *Here are a number of the smaller vent animals, including two types of crabs, a small clam, and a sea-living worm.*

FORESTS OF THE SEA

Most of the sea's plant life is made up of the microscopic plant plankton that grows in the sunlit upper layers. But in some shallow, warm waters, sea is the perfect place for large underwater plants to grow.

Underwater "forests" are not made from trees and bushes, but from giant seaweeds or other marine plants. In this undersea greenery live special animals – either browsing on the plants or eating smaller animals that make their homes there.

There are three main sorts of underwater forest. The first is found on shallow, sandy sea bottoms near the land. This is made from huge areas of a plant called eelgrass. The eelgrass beds are really better called fields than forests because the plants look like slim-leaved grasses.

The two other sorts of plants really do make forests. They are made from giant seaweed kelps. Off the coast of California are kelps that are anchored to the sea bottom. In the Sargasso Sea, located in the North Atlantic, there are forests of seaweed – sargassum weed – that is never rooted to the ocean floor, but floats with the movement of the sea.

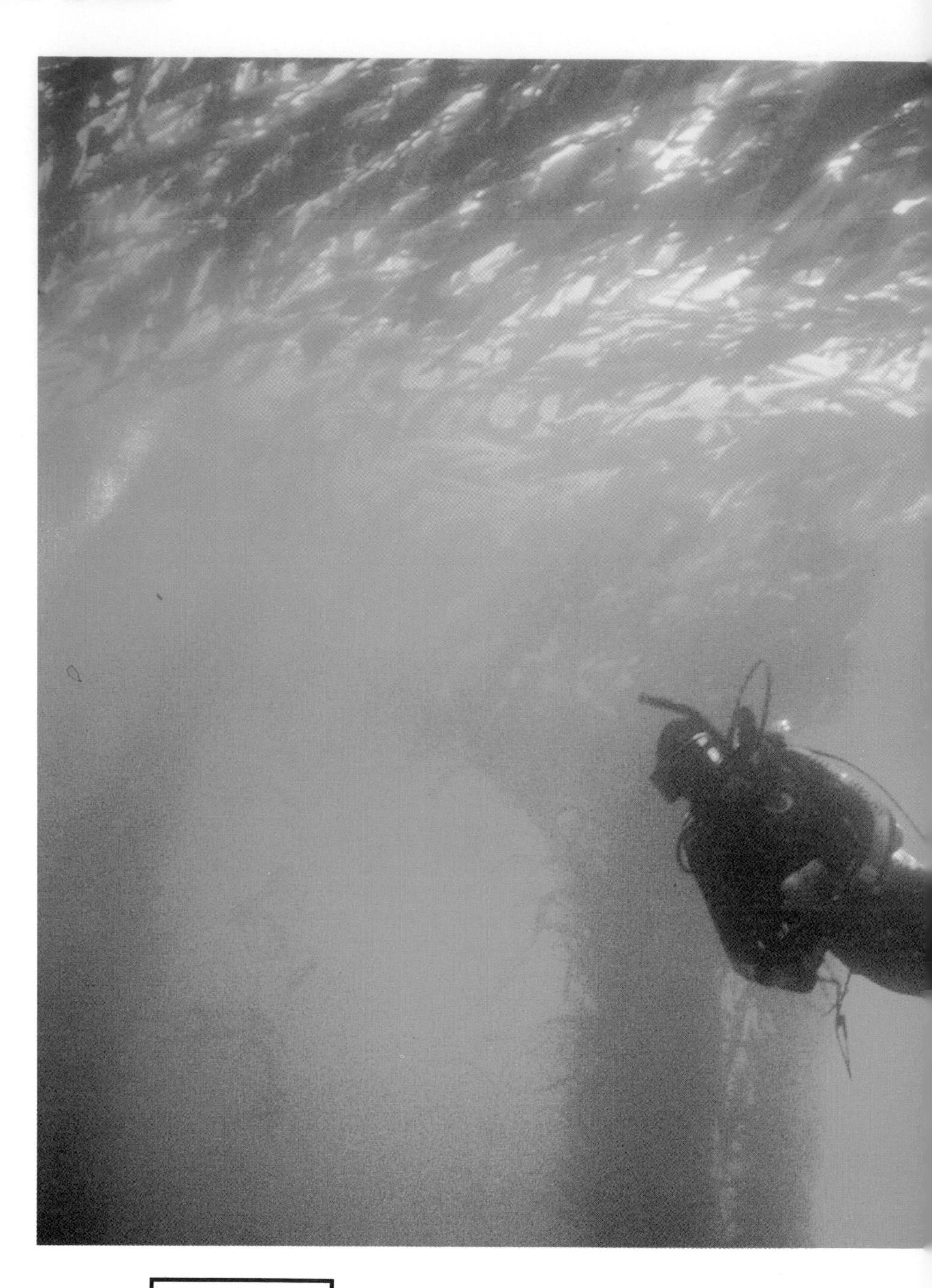

FACT FILE

The fastest – growing plants in the world are giant kelps. In warm water they can grow a staggering 24 inches (60 cm) in just one day!

Dugongs are large, seal-like mammals with a tail like a fish. They feed on kelp beds and eelgrass underwater.

Eelgrasses are the only undersea plants with real leaves and roots like land plants. At the right time of the year, they even have tiny underwater flowers.

Marine iguanas are the only sea-going lizards. They live on the lava rocks off the shores of the Galapagos Islands. To get their food, they dive to the sea bottom and eat seaweed.

Sea hares are not underwater rabbits, but sea slugs with tentacles like a hare's ears. They browse on the surface of kelp plants.

◀ *Under a dappled canopy of giant kelp seaweed plants, a diver swims through an underwater forest off the coast of California.*

▲ *This close-up photograph shows how the giant kelp plants stay more or less upright in strong currents. Their fronds are kept afloat with gas-filled bladders.*

► *A kelp snail is a plant eater. This one crawls steadily over the surface of a giant kelp plant. It uses a fine-toothed tongue to scrape off the surface of the kelp for food,.*

DIVING FOR FOOD

Sea otters live in kelp beds and feed on fish and shellfish, called abalones. They dive for the abalones, bring them to the surface, and crack them open on a rock which they hold on their chest.

FROZEN SEAS

In the polar regions at the top (north) and bottom (south) of our planet, it gets cold enough for seawater to freeze. In fact, the whole of the mass of ice which we call the Arctic, with the North Pole at its center, is not a continent of land at all. Instead, it is a huge raft of floating ice made out of frozen seawater. When the sea freezes like this, we call it pack ice.

However, the Antarctic, with the South Pole at its center, is different. It is a real land continent covered with a very thick layer of glacier ice, built up from snow.

Icebergs are individual chunks of ice floating in the sea. Pieces of pack ice may break off from the main sheets and form flattish icebergs. They are made of seawater ice. The jagged icebergs, that look like mountains floating in the sea, are pieces of land ice from glaciers that slip into the sea. They come from frozen snow and are therefore made of fresh water.

The unfrozen seawaters close to the ice sheets of the polar regions are rich in the minerals that help plankton grow well. This ensures these waters are teeming with animal life as well.

▲ *Like a beautiful fairy castle of ice, only one-tenth of an iceberg shows above water. The remaining nine-tenths are beneath the surface.*

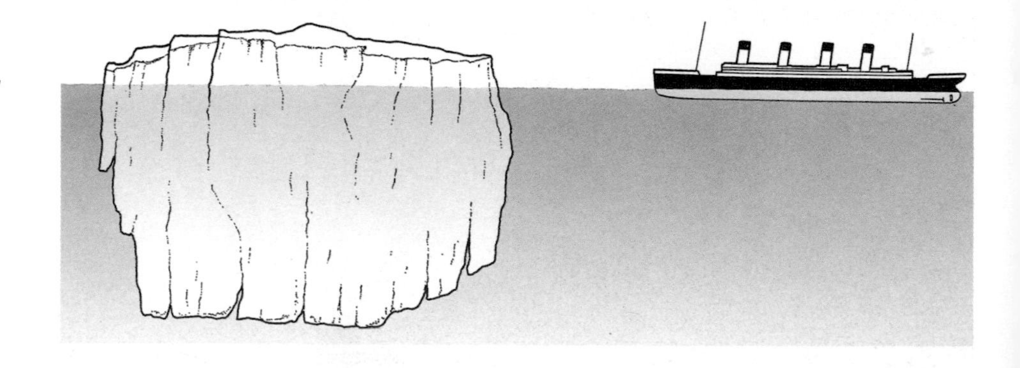

► *Icebergs can sink ships. The most famous example was the ocean liner* Titanic, *which went down in the Atlantic after hitting an iceberg on its first voyage in 1912.*

◀ *Polar bears are the top predators on the pack ice of the Arctic Ocean. They are at home in the icy water as well as moving about on the ice. They eat seals, fish, and seabirds in winter and add berries and leaves to their diets in summer.*

FACT FILE

Freezing facts. Although fresh water freezes at 32°F/0°C, the salts in seawater keep it from freezing into ice until it is cooled to about 28.4°F/−2°C.

Icebergs in the desert. Some scientists have suggested that icebergs would be a useful source of water in the desert areas of the world – if they could be towed fast enough so they didn't melt on the way.

Icefish are a weird family of fish that live on the bottom of the Antarctic Ocean. They are the only backboned animals that do not have red blood. Instead, it is whitish or colorless. In the freezing cold of the sea bottom, icefish have no use for red blood cells. The oxygen they need is dissolved instead of being carried by the red blood cells as it is in other fish.

Antarctica is a land without land animals except a few tiny insects. All the large animals on the Antarctic ice are sea animals like seals and penguins.

The Arctic is made up of a thick layer of frozen seawater. Atomic-powered submarines can travel from one side to the other in the water below the pack ice.

Emperor penguins are the world's largest penguins. They stand 4 feet (over 1 meter) tall, and both males and females have bright yellow feathers around their necks.

Icefish

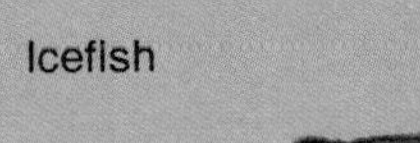

▲ *The emperor penguin breeds on pack ice and islands around Antarctica. The female lays one egg which the male carries on his warm feet for two months until it hatches. During this time, the female goes to sea to feed.*

DIVING INTO DARKNESS

People are air-breathing animals, and can only hold their breath for a few minutes at a time. Because of these problems, people have always needed diving equipment and diving machines to explore the undersea world.

The earliest diving suits were little more than barrels which fitted over a person's head and body. The barrel was sealed with leather flaps, had a glass viewing plate so the diver could see out, and was joined by an air hose to the surface. To keep the diver alive, a hand pump pushed air down the hose so that he could breathe.

Later diving suits were all-enclosing clothes of rubber with lead-weighted boots. The diver's head was encased in a brass helmet with thick glass portholes. Air was pumped down to the diver under high pressure using a mechanical pump.

Modern underwater exploration is done by divers who wear scuba (Self-Contained Underwater Breathing Apparatus) gear, or by the mini-submarines called submersibles.

The great advantage of scuba diving – with flippers, a wet-suit, face-mask, and air stored in bottles – is that the divers can go anywhere they wish (down to a safe depth) without being attached to the surface by an air hose.

◀ Diving under the sea has always been a dangerous business. This print shows divers in diving suits with air lines trying to save the lives of the crew of a submarine wreck in 1905.

▼ Compressed air tanks, carried on the back, keep today's scuba divers alive while they explore underwater. Equipped like this, a diver can investigate underwater life.

◀ Air was pumped from the surface to the wearer of this diving barrel 200 years ago. Only short dives at shallow water depths were possible with this equipment.

FACT FILE

Modern divers, going to great depths, breathe not compressed air, but a safer mixture of compressed oxygen and helium. It makes their voices sound squeaky like cartoon characters!

For safety's sake, divers must avoid coming to the surface from deep dives too quickly. If they come up too fast, they can get "the bends." This is a dangerous condition in which gas bubbles form in the blood. The bubbles are like those which fizz out of carbonated soda when you open the can.

In 1878, the self-contained diving suit was invented. For the first time, a diver could work under the sea without being joined to the surface by an air pipe.

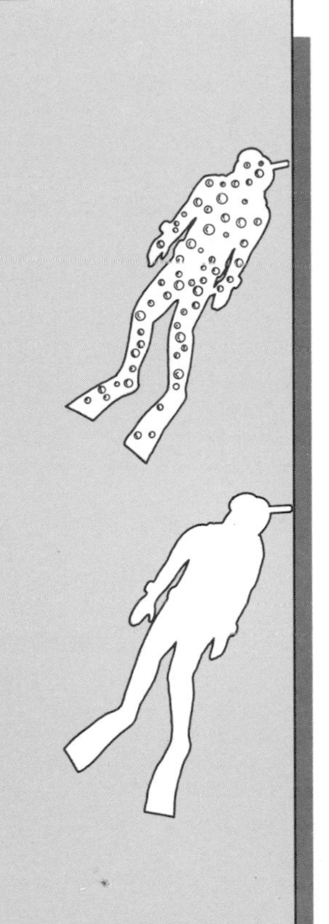

Pearl fishers dive to about 40 feet (12 meters) using no artificial air supply.

Scuba divers with bottles of compressed air can go down to about 200 feet (60 meters).

Helmet divers, breathing a mixture of helium and oxygen to avoid "the bends," dive to 820 feet (250 meters).

Commercial minisubs can be used for repairs on offshore oil fields to a depth of 1,500 feet (457 meters).

Research submersibles can go down to 3,000–5,000 feet (915–1,520 meters) to study the sea bottom.

A bathyscaphe is a research submersible with a steel globe to protect the scientists from the great pressures of the sea. It can go to the sea's deepest depths, over 35,000 feet (10,668 meters) down.

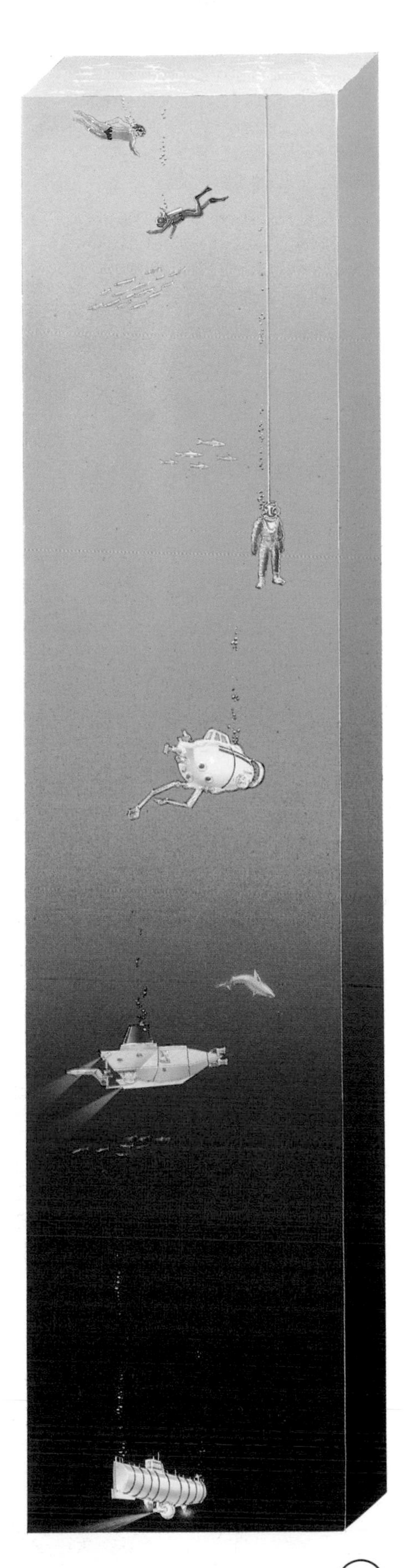

UNDERWATER TRAVEL

For hundreds of years people have tried to make an undersea boat. The design of such a boat, or submarine as it is usually called, has two big problems. How will the people who travel in it get enough air to breathe? How is it possible to stop the air-filled part of the submarine getting squashed flat by the heavy pressure of the seawater?

The air problem has been solved by taking down a supply of compressed air that can be piped into the cabin for the crew. The pressure problem in submarines is solved by building the hull of the craft out of thick, strong metal that can stand up to the heavy pressure of the sea.

Today, there are two types of submarines – ordinary submarines and submersibles. Submarines are large and designed to slip easily through the water. They can hold as many as 150 people and travel at speeds up to 40 miles per hour (64 kilometers per hour). Submersibles have a very small, air-filled hull holding only two or three crew members.

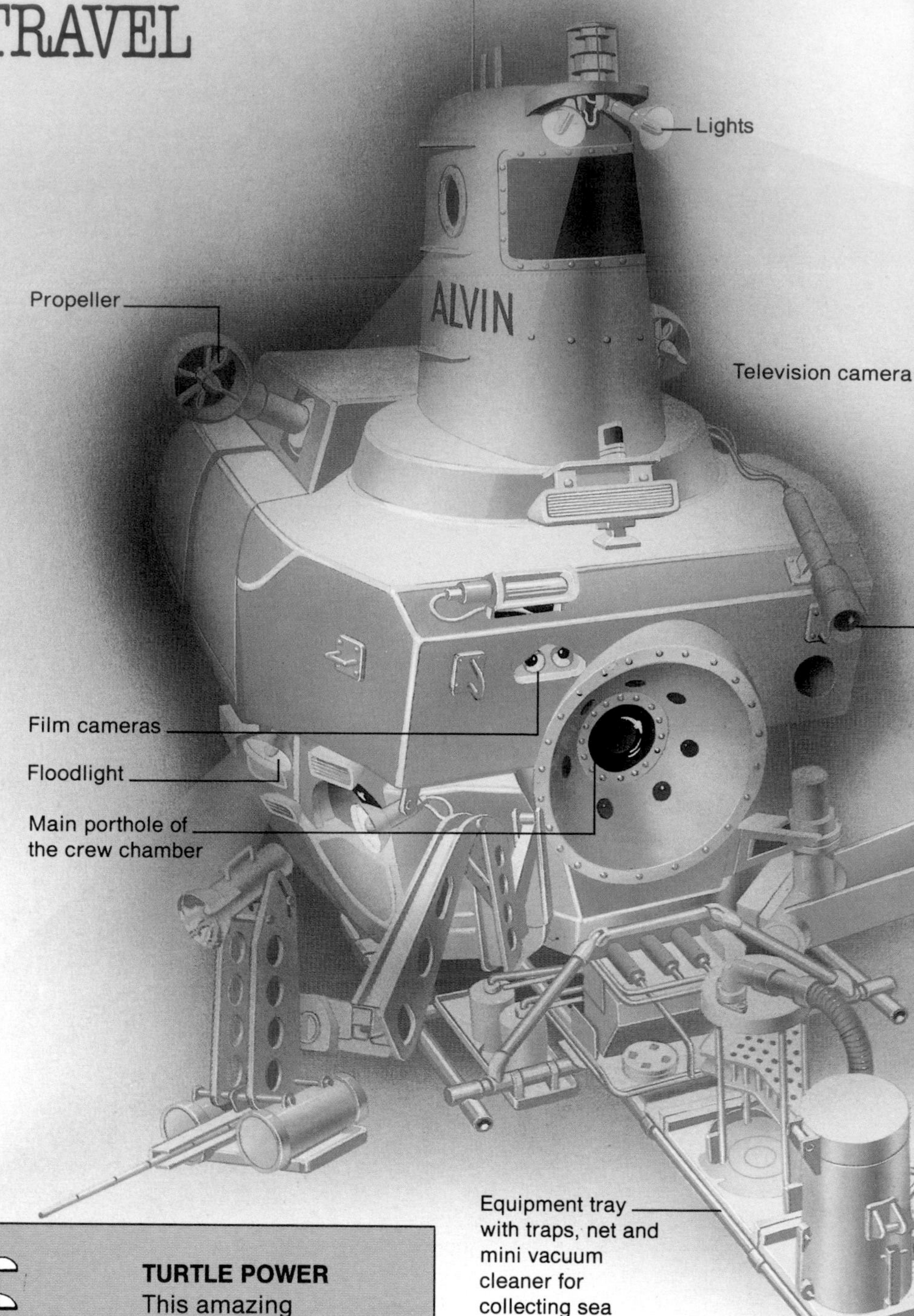

▲ *The* Alvin *is a very good example of a modern research submersible which can go down about 13,000 feet (4,000 meters) below the sea. All the crew members are safe inside a strong, round chamber with thick glass windows. The rest of the craft is machinery for making* Alvin *go up or down, moving it about slowly, and for collecting or photographing objects on the seabed.*

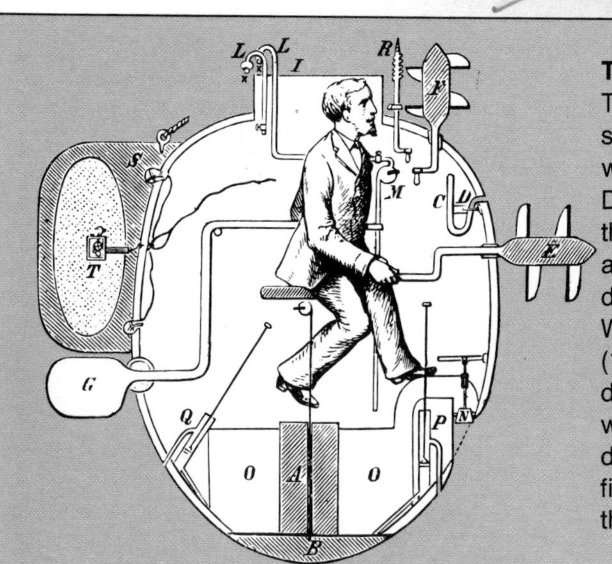

TURTLE POWER
This amazing submarine, the *Turtle*, was built in 1776 by David Bushnell in the United States to attack British ships during the American War of Independence (1775–1781). It was driven by one man who also had the dangerous job of fixing explosives to the enemy ships.

▲ *The Johnson* Sea Link *submersible and its mother ship. The* Sea Link's *special feature is a chamber made out of very thick, clear plastic. It means the crew has a good view when underwater.*

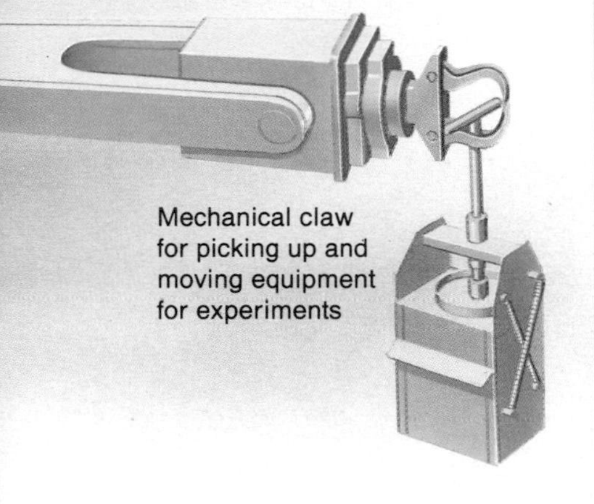

Mechanical claw for picking up and moving equipment for experiments

FACT FILE

In the year 400 BC, Alexander the Great is reported to have gone under the sea in an early diving bell.

In 1863, the early submarine named *David* was used in the American Civil War between the North and South. It was the first submarine ever to sink an enemy ship.

Space metal. The crew's chamber in the *Alvin* submersible is made out of the incredibly strong metal called titanium, which is also used for making spacecraft.

Alvin was the submersible used to take underwater photographs and video film of the wreck of the *Titanic* on the floor of the Atlantic Ocean.

Deepest dive. The *Trieste* submersible has dived as deep as it is possible to go – 36,000 feet (11,000 meters) to the bottom of the Pacific Ocean. To get down to that depth, it carried nine tons of iron pellets on board. When it needed to rise back to the surface the iron pellets were dropped so that it floated up again.

► *The Perry Cubmarine is a mix between a small submarine and a submersible. It has a larger hull than an ordinary submersible and can carry more crew members.*

WRECKS!

The bottoms of the oceans are like a vast dump, littered with the remains of wrecked ships. Sailing the seas and oceans has always been dangerous.

Even today – with radar, radios, good weather forecasts, and satellite-based navigation equipment that can tell a ship's captain where he is in the world – ships still sink. They collide in the dark. They run into icebergs and reefs. They go down in huge waves during storms or they are sunk during battles. It was even more dangerous to travel at sea in the past, when there was no help except perhaps a simple compass for direction.

Wrecks on the seabed are always fascinating. Sometimes they are searched out because of tales about rich treasures on board. Other ancient ones are investigated by underwater explorers because the wrecks are like undersea museums.

A 3,000-year-old shipwreck will be full of things that can tell us about the lives of people who lived many hundreds of years ago. We can tell what the cargo was, whether the ship used sails or oars, what equipment the crew took to sea with them, and whether it was a fighting ship or a trading one. No wonder divers are always looking for wrecks.

► *The remains of the* Mary Rose *were recovered from the seabed in 1982.*

▼ *A collection of gold coins found on the* Mary Rose. *Each one was worth about a quarter at that time. This was enough to pay a sailor for a month.*

FACT FILE

Jason Junior is the unlikely name of a remote-controlled deep-sea robot camera system. It was used to take pictures around and inside the wreck of the *Titanic* on the bed of the Atlantic Ocean.

SONAR is a sort of underwater radar. It works by sound waves "pinging" out from a ship – bouncing off the seabed – and being reflected back to the ship again. It is used for finding wrecks on the seabed.

An underwater computer was developed in Australia in 1986. It means divers can record what they find immediately.

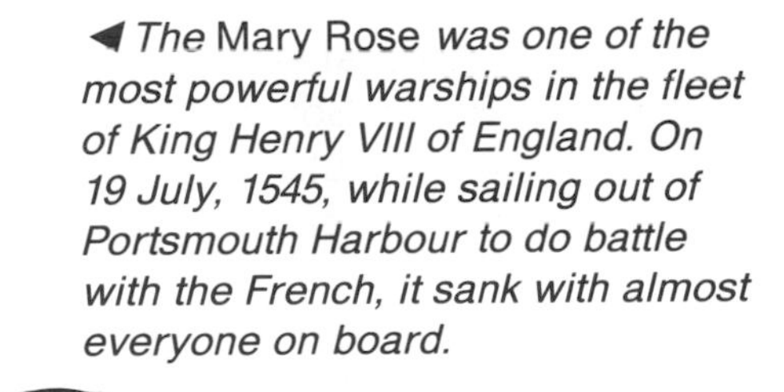

◀ *The* Mary Rose *was one of the most powerful warships in the fleet of King Henry VIII of England. On 19 July, 1545, while sailing out of Portsmouth Harbour to do battle with the French, it sank with almost everyone on board.*

▼ *The divers in this photograph are searching for treasure from the wreck of the* Tolosa. *This ship was sunk by a hurricane on August 24, 1724, off the coast of Central America. It was sailing from Portugal to Mexico on a royal mission, and carried 1,200 passengers as well as cargo. Hundreds of valuable items were retrieved from the wreck.*

SOS in Morse code (. . . – – – . . .) is used as a distress signal at sea. It first saved lives when two steamers picked up an SOS from the shipwrecked liner *Slavonia* in 1909.

A good vintage! Some of the pottery wine containers found in ancient Greek shipwrecks were so well sealed that they still have wine in them after 2,000 years.

HARVEST OF THE SEA

Each year, more than 70 million tons of fish are caught in the world's oceans. The size and depth of the oceans is so vast that the success of sea fishermen is amazing. Most fishing methods, though, are very simple and have hardly changed since people first got their food from the sea many thousands of years ago.

In their search for fish – the "wild animals" of the sea – most fishermen use some sort of net, or they use hooks with bait on which the fish get caught as they try to eat the bait. Fishermen may trick fish nearer to the surface by shining a bright light onto the water, or they may lure crabs and lobsters into special pots left on rocky sea bottoms. In the most advanced fishing boats, echo-sounding equipment is used to find the fish.

When nets are used, they may be left floating in the water so that fish swimming near the surface become caught in them. They are called gill nets. Purse seines are like huge, circular net bags with a drawstring. The school of fish is surrounded by the net. Then the drawstring is pulled together to trap the fish inside the closed "purse."

Drag, or trawl, nets work quite differently. The trawl is a long netting bag which is open at one end only. It is pulled along the sea floor by powerful fishing boats called trawlers. The open end of the bag catches fish in the same way as a giant net catches butterflies on land.

Fishing by these methods works very well. In fact, it works so well that sometimes fish are caught before they have a chance to breed and increase their numbers. This "overfishing" means that stocks of certain fish have become dangerously low.

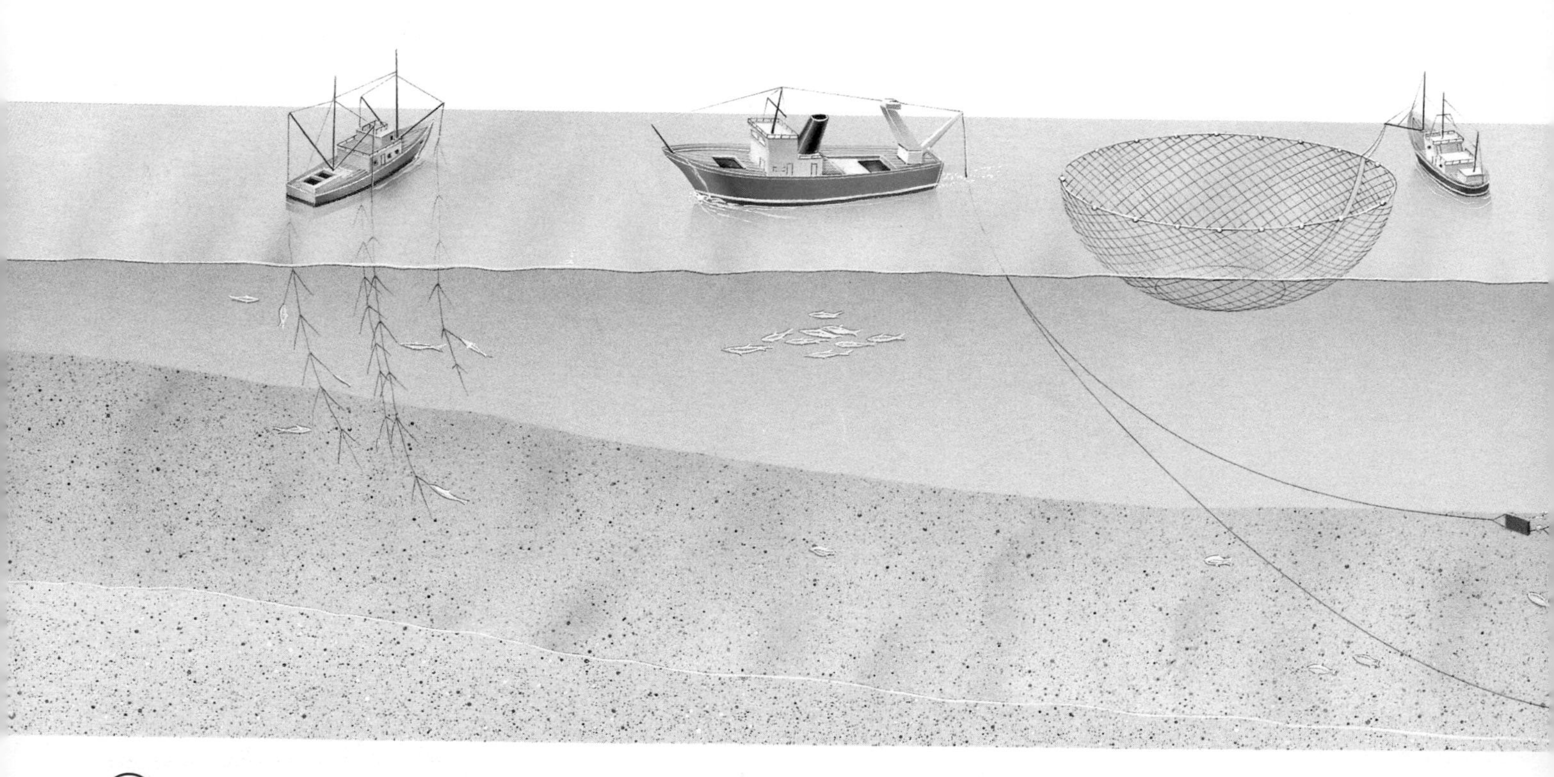

◀ This huge catch of mackerel is the result of modern fishing in European waters off the Faeroe Islands.

◀ These are the traditional boats of people who live in a fishing village in Kerala, on the coast of southern India.

◀ From left to right are shown four different ways of catching large numbers of fish at sea.
Long-line fishing: *long fishing lines with thousands of baited hooks.*
Trawling: *a bag-shaped net is being dragged along the seabed.*
Purse-seining: *fish are trapped in a circular net with floats at the top.*
Gill-netting: *a long wall of netting floats in the water to entangle fish.*

FACT FILE

The biggest catch of fish was an estimated 120 million fish caught in one purse seine.

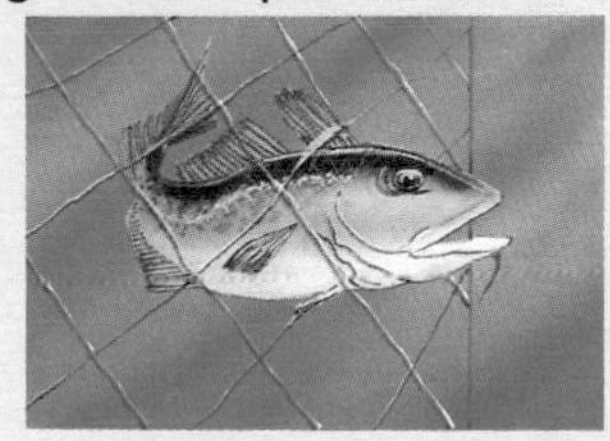

Many countries control the sizes of fish that can be caught by having laws about the size of the holes in their nets. If the hole is large enough, young fish can escape and breed to produce more fish.

An American lobster measuring $3\frac{1}{2}$ feet (just over 1 meter) was caught off the coast of Canada.

FARMING FOR FISH

In addition to catching wild fish with boats at sea, it is also possible to farm sea life, just as we breed cows and sheep, and grow wheat on land. Sea farming fish and shellfish, and plants like seaweed, is called aquaculture.

Fish farming has gone on for many hundreds of years with freshwater fish like carp and catfish in ponds. More recently, the same idea has been used for sea fish. It has been a great success. Now, for instance, much of the salmon sold in Britain does not come from fish caught in the wild, but from fish farmed in huge cages in Scottish sea lochs.

This way of getting sea fish is quite different from ordinary fishing. In one way, it is a much easier method. Fishermen do not have to go hunting for the fish – they are swimming around in a huge cage. The fish farmer can take fish from the cage when they are needed.

The problem with fish farming is that it is expensive, because large amounts of food have to be put in the cages to make the fish grow to a useful size.

Shellfish like mussels and oysters can also be farmed in shallow seawater. Special oysters can also be grown to make pearls to use in jewelry. Shrimp, crabs, and lobsters can also be farmed in the same way. So, too, can seaweed.

► *People prefer to use natural products rather than artificial ones. Today, substances from seaweed help to thicken ice cream, milk shakes, face creams, and soups. They are also used in the manufacture of photographic film, cotton thread, medicines, and paint.*

▼ *These floating rafts at Kyushu in Japan are used for growing the shells of oysters for making cultivated pearls. They look just like natural pearls but are much cheaper.*

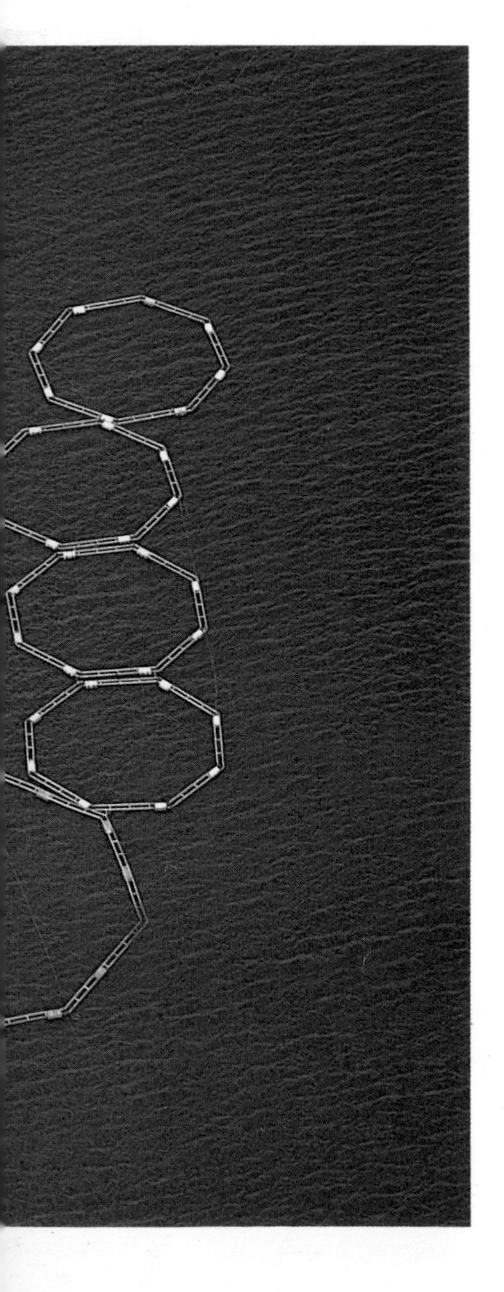

FACT FILE

Ice cream keeps its shape because it is thickened with a special substance made from seaweed.

In Wales, a natural seaweed is eaten as a traditional food – it is called "laver bread."

A cultivated pearl can only be told from a naturally grown one by looking at it under an X-ray machine!

A commercial shrimp farm can grow 65,000 pounds (about 30,000 kg) of shrimp each year, starting with eggs obtained from wild female shrimp.

People in Japan eat more seaweed than anywhere else in the world. They call it *nori* and cultivate several different kinds in shallow coastal seas.

MINING THE SEA

Mining for coal, metal ores, or other minerals, and digging wells for oil are all things that you expect to happen on land. As more and more of these materials are used, though, the amounts remaining to be dug out of the ground on land get smaller and smaller. Because of this problem, engineers have started to search in the seabed for new supplies.

So far, the most important materials mined this way are natural gas and oil. They are called fossil fuels because they are made from the fossilized remains of animals and plants that lived and died millions of years ago.

When there are supplies of gas and oil under the seabed, holes have to be drilled down into them. This drilling can go on either from a special ship with a drill mounted on it, or from an oil well that sits on the seabed but sticks up into the air. Oil and gas from them can either be pumped along pipes to the nearest land or put into tankers which then carry it to a port.

Other minerals can be mined from the sea as well. The simplest to get is sea salt. In many parts of the world, saltwater in shallow lakes near the sea is allowed to dry up in the Sun until only the salt is left. There are also plans in the future to scoop up the lumps of metal-rich minerals that cover the seabed in some oceans. These lumps – called nodules – have rare metals like manganese in them.

▼ *This huge oil well in the sea is called Statfjord B. It was placed in the North Sea halfway between Norway (where it was built) and the Shetland Islands off Scotland in 1981. It is so big it can stand steadily on the seabed, held there by its gigantic weight of over 800,000 tons. From this "oil production platform" as it is called, 32 separate wells have been drilled. Oil comes up from them into the platform.*

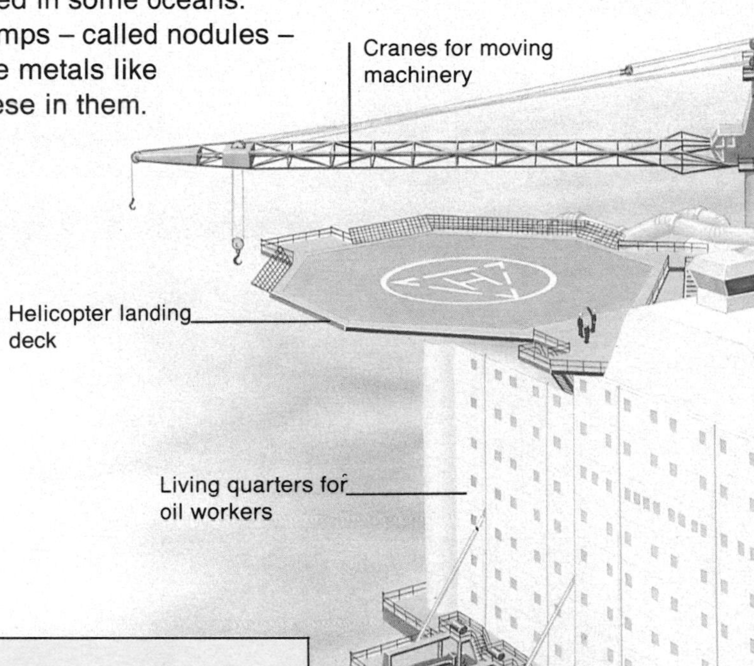

FACT FILE

The Statfjord B platform is shown in this picture alongside buildings in Manhattan. You can see that the massive legs that hold up the platform are taller than the United Nations Building.

The platform is the heaviest man-made object that has ever been moved. It is made of nearly a million tons of steel and concrete.

The cost of the platform when it was built was almost two billion dollars.

150,000 barrels of oil a day can be taken from the seabed when the platform works flat out.

The drills can bore down almost 20,000 feet (6,100 meters) into the seabed rocks.

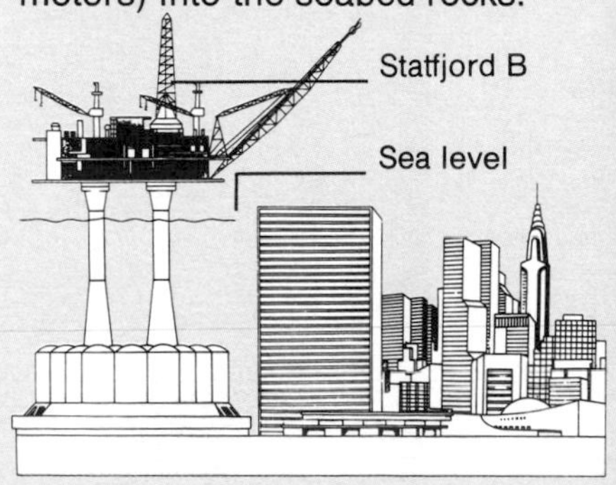

OIL ORIGINS

Oil forms, deep in the Earth's rocks, from the fossilized remains of ancient plankton. Over many millions of years, this plankton was changed by pressure and heat into pockets of oil and gas.

Index

BIBLIOGRAPHY

Saving the Whale, M. Burton, Franklin Watts, London and New York, 1989
Creatures of the Deep, *Life on a Coral Reef*, *Whales and Dolphins*, L. Bender, Franklin Watts, London and New York, 1989
The Vanishing Manatee, M. G. Clark, Cobblehill Books, New York, 1990
Sharks, S. & R. Coupe, Facts on File Inc, New York 1990
Whales, L. Dow, Facts on File Inc, New York, 1990
The Usborne Book of Ocean Facts, A. Ganeri, Usborne Publishing Ltd, London, 1990
Dolphins and Porpoises, J. Hatherly, & D. Nicholls, Facts on File Inc, London, 1990
The Young Scientist Book of the Undersea, C. Pick, Usborne Publishing Ltd, London, Rev. Ed. 1982
Usborne Mysteries and Marvels of Ocean Life, R. Morris, Usborne Publishing Ltd, London, 1983
Just Look at . . . Life in the Sea, B. Stonehouse, Macdonald & Co, (Publishers) Ltd, 1984

PHOTOGRAPH CREDITS

1 **Ron and Valerie Taylor/Ardea London;** 2–3 **Konrad Wothe/Frank Lane Picture Agency;** 4 **Soames Summerhays/Biofotos;** 5 **Ron and Valerie Taylor/Ardea London;** 6–7 **Georgette Douwma/Planet Earth Pictures;** 7 **Bruce Coleman:** *top* **Jane Burton,** *bottom* **N. Fox-Davies;** 8 **Soames Summerhays/Biofotos;** 9 *left* **S. Jonasson/Frank Lane Picture Agency,** *right* **Tony Waltham;** 10 **Jane Burton/Bruce Coleman;** 11 **Bruce Coleman:** *top* **N. Fox-Davies,** *bottom* **Jane Burton;** 12 **D. P. Wilson/Eric and David Hosking;** 16 **Carl Roessler/Planet Earth Pictures;** 17 **Peter David/Planet Earth Pictures;** 18 *bottom* **Peter David/Planet Earth Pictures;** 18–19 **Georgette Douwma/Planet Earth Pictures;** 19 **Planet Earth Pictures:** *top* **Herwarth Voigtmann,** *bottom* **Peter Scoones;** 20 **David George/Planet Earth Pictures;** 21 **Ron and Valerie Taylor/Ardea London;** 22 *top* **Oxford Scientific Films,** *bottom* **Ian Took/Biofotos:** 24 **Soames Summerhays/Biofotos;** 25 *top* **Bill Wood/Natural History Photographic Agency,** *bottom* **F. Jack Jackson/Robert Harding Picture Library;** 27 *top* **David Woodfall/Natural History Photographic Agency,** *bottom* **Bruce Coleman;** 28 *top* **Rudie H. Kuiter/Oxford Scientific Films,** *bottom* **Robert Arnold/Planet Earth Pictures;** 29 **Rudie H. Kuiter;** 30 **Heather Angel;** 31 **Masahiro Iijima/Ardea London;** 33 **Marty Snyderman/Planet Earth Pictures;** 34 *top* **Soames Summerhays/Biofotos,** *inset* **Planet Earth Pictures;** 34–5 **Ron and Valerie Taylor/Ardea London;** 37 **François Gohier/Ardea London;** 38 *left* **S. McCutcheon/Frank Lane Picture Agency;** 38–39 **Barbara Todd/Natural History Photographic Agency;** 39 **François Gohier/Ardea London,** *bottom* **Heather Angel;** 40 **John Lythgoe/Planet Earth Pictures;** 41 **Frank Lane Picture Agency;** 42–43 **D. P. Wilson/Eric and David Hosking;** 44 **Sygma-Paris;** 45 **Planet Earth Pictures;** 47 *top* **Bruce Coleman Limited,** *inset* **Frank Lane Picture Agency;** 48 **Soames Summerhays/Biofotos;** 49 *both* **Ron and Valerie Taylor/Ardea London;** 50, 51 *top* and *centre* **Ron and Valerie Taylor/Ardea London,** 51 *bottom* **Carl Roessler/Bruce Coleman;** 52–53 **Robert Hessler/Planet Earth Pictures;** 54–55 **Norbert Wu/Planet Earth Pictures;** 55 *inset* **Bruce Coleman;** 56 **C. Carvalho/Frank Lane Picture Agency;** 57 **Bryan and Cherry Alexander;** 58 **Ann Ronan Picture Library;** 58–59 **Christian Petron/Planet Earth Pictures;** 60 **Mary Evans Picture Library;** 61 *top left* **Dr. Roland Emson,** *top right* **Tom Smoyer/Harbor Branch Oceanographic Institution;** *bottom* **Flip Schulke/Planet Earth Pictures;** 62 **Adam Woolfitt/Susan Griggs Agency,** *inset* **Tim Francis/Planet Earth Pictures;** 63 **Jonathan Blair/Susan Griggs Agency;** 64–65 **Gerald Cubitt/Bruce Coleman Limited;** 65 **Alastair Scott/Susan Griggs Agency;** 66 **Dr. Georg Gerster/The John Hillelson Agency;** 67 **Ivaldi/Jerrican.**

ARTWORK CREDITS

8, 19, 62–63, 69 **John Hutchinson;** 8–9, 10–11, 16–17, 40–41, 46–47, 52–53 **Pavel Kostal;** 12–13, 14–15, 20–21, 26–27, 32–33, 57 (bottom) **Colin Newman;** 21, 23, 25, 28, 37, 45 **Paul Richardson;** 30–31 maps, 67 **Ed Stuart;** 31 green turtle **Alan Male;** 31 line artwork 33 (top) **Michael Woods;** line artworks 33 (bottom), 38, 41, 55, 56, 58, 63 **Rhoda and Robert Burns;** 42–43, 48, 59, 64–65 **Guy Smith;** 49 **Tony Graham;** 57 Penguin **Peter Hayman;** 60–61, 68–69 **Trevor Hill.**